How could she take that first step beyond her fears?

Once at the door, all thought of the amicable stranger fled. For as the automatic door swung open she saw, just beyond it, that a huge German shepherd was sitting, waiting.

Her pulse began to race as she tried to block out the nightmarish images from the past, images that threatened to paralyze her with fear.

Yet all she blocked out was the present, the bustle of the store, the rain spitting against the wide glass window, until it seemed the only reality was the big dog waiting on the other side of the door.

This is silly, she scolded herself. *I can't stand here forever, half blocking the door. The dog isn't going to bother me.*

Dogs were her phobia, a phobia she seemed powerless to overcome.

"Do you need some help?" a voice intruded into her feelings of despair. It was the man from the express lane. His brow furrowed with concern. "Are you sick?"

Only with humiliation. She stammered, "N-no. It's . . . it's the dog."

He glanced through the glass door and back. "What about the dog?"

Her eyes drew tears. She blinked to hold them back. "Could you . . . do you think you could make him go away?"

"But he isn't going to hurt you."

His reasonable tone made matters worse. Hating her own helplessness, Mandy backed further from the door.

HEART AFLAME

Susan Kirby

Serenade/Serenata
BOOKS
of the Zondervan Publishing House
Grand Rapids, Michigan

A Note From The Author:
I love to hear from my readers! You may correspond with me by writing:

     Susan Kirby
     1415 Lake Drive, S.E.
     Grand Rapids, MI 49506

HEART AFLAME
Copyright © 1985 by Susan Kirby

Serenade/Serenata is an imprint of
The Zondervan Publishing House
1415 Lake Drive, S.E.
Grand Rapids, Michigan 49506

ISBN 0-310-46902-3

Printed in the United States of America

86 87 88 89 90 / 10 9 8 7 6 5 4 3 2 1

To Niki

CHAPTER 1

THERE WERE DAYS WHEN Mandy Holt wondered what possessed her to believe she could carry on her career as a seamstress out of her home. Today was one. The interruptions had been endless.

She pushed away from the table and reached for the phone, her "Hello?" all but a sigh.

"Are you by chance going to the store, Dear?"

Recognizing the voice of her elderly neighbor across the hall, Mandy hadn't the heart to say a trip to the store wasn't on her agenda. Rather, she murmured, "Was there something you needed, Miss Princeton?"

"All this rain makes poor Willie restless. You know how he eats when he's restless. I've just run out of food and already he's sniffing his empty dish and meowing reproaches at me."

Privately, Mandy doubted starvation was imminent. Willie was the fattest yellow tabby she'd ever seen. But knowing Ida Princeton wouldn't see it that way, Mandy said, "Give me ten minutes, Miss Princeton. I want to finish a row of stay-stitching, then I'll run to the store."

"Oh, my. You're sewing," Ida fretted. "Forgive me for interrupting, child. I'll go myself."

"No, I don't mind," Mandy insisted, disliking the thought of Ida out on rain-slick streets inviting a fall. "Ten minutes, then I'll go."

True to her word, Mandy was into her rain coat and out the door in short order. The gloomy spring drizzle outside her apartment building was cold on her face, yet because Danny's Market was only two blocks away, walking seemed as quick as driving.

She tugged up the hood of her jacket, mindless of the copper-brown curls that curled up close to frame her heart-shaped face. The sprint in the rain seemed to blow cobwebs from her mind, and all in all, she decided the water-spots on the hem of her slacks were worth her fresh outlook on the day.

Danny's was doing a brisk business. Mandy whisked past other shoppers, grabbed the cat food and headed for the express lane. A dowdy-haired woman cut in front of her, aiming a heavy-laden cart into the lane marked, "Ten Items Or Less."

Trying to practice patience, a virtue she hadn't quite mastered, Mandy resisted giving the inconsiderate woman a "Can't you read?" look, and scanned the magazine rack instead.

Behind her a deep voice made the cheery observation, "Nice day for ducks, isn't it?"

Mandy turned, a quiet smile shaping her mouth. "Isn't it though?" She was about to turn back, but there was a vitality about the man which held her a second longer. Shallow dimples framing a straight line of a mouth deepened in a return smile, and detecting a mutual spark of interest, Mandy felt her pulse quicken.

His smoky grey eyes scrutinized hers without giving much in return. "*Express lane. Ten Items Or Less.* What a waste of a sign," he said, gaze shifting from the overhead sign to the lady in front of Mandy who was still emptying her cart onto the check-out counter.

Mandy hoped he wasn't going to get rude about the woman because rudeness in him would have been a disappointment. Without thinking her motives through, she sought to forestall him.

"If you're in a hurry, you're welcome to go in front of me."

Surprise, then chagrin crossed his tanned features. He ran a sun-bronzed hand through dark brown hair that waved back from a low forehead then settled half covering his ears.

"I wasn't hinting," he said. "It's just kind of ironic how we all fly for the fast lane, then end up on idle."

His grin was irresistible. Mandy chuckled and admitted, "You're right. I feel as if I've been racing hard all morning and all I've managed to achieve is to fall further behind."

"You aren't alone," he consoled. "That's about the size of my morning, too."

They talked a moment longer, until Mandy's attention was required by the cashier. She paid for the cat food, then started for the door, suddenly very conscious of the way she took her steps, as if the man might be watching her.

Yet once at the door, all thought of the amicable stranger fled. For as the automatic door swung open, she saw, just beyond it, a huge German shepherd sat waiting.

Hastily she retreated inside. Her pulse began to race as she tried to block out the nightmarish images from the past, images that threatened to paralyze her with fear.

Yet all she blocked out was the present, the bustle of the store, the rain spitting against the wide glass window, until it seemed the only reality was the big dog waiting on the other side of the door.

From far away an impatient voice snapped, "Excuse me." Before Mandy could step aside, a woman brushed by carrying groceries and dragging a child along by the hand.

Mandy surfaced as if out of a trance. She watched the woman and child pass the dog without incident. *This is silly*, she scolded herself. *I can't stand here forever, half blocking the door. The dog didn't bother them. He isn't going to bother me, either.*

Dogs were her phobia, a phobia she seemed powerless to overcome, and she lacked the fortitude to take that first step beyond her fears.

"Do you need some help?" a voice intruded into her feelings of despair. It was the man from the express lane. His brow furrowed with concern. "Are you sick?"

Only with humiliation. She stammered, "N-no. It's . . . it's the dog."

He glanced through the glass door and back. "What about the dog?"

Her eyes drew tears. She blinked to hold them back. "I . . . I'm afraid of dogs. Could you . . . do you think you could make him go away?"

"But he isn't going to hurt you."

His reasonable tone, soothing yet accusing too, made matters worse. Hating her own helplessness, Mandy backed further from the door.

"I'd imagine he's waiting for his master," the man went on in that adult-to-child tone he had adopted. "I'm certain he won't pay any attention to you."

Wishing the floor would open up and swallow her, Mandy tightened her grip on the sack. "In my head, I know you're right. But I can't make the rest of me believe it."

"You're that scared?" His voice was frankly bewildered.

Fresh color flooding her cheeks, Mandy nodded.

He paused a moment, as if debating, then took charge of the situation by shifting his own sack of groceries and offering his free arm. "I'll walk you past the dog. All the way to your car, if that will help."

"I didn't drive a car," Mandy forced out the words.

"Then there's nothing to keep me from driving you home, is there?"

She grabbed at his arm like a lifeline. "I'd really appreciate it. My apartment isn't far."

If he thought her an unforgivable coward, his smile didn't betray it. Staying between her and the dog, he lead her out into the parking lot.

"This is it." He pointed out a car, quietly elegant and undeniably expensive.

He held the door and she slipped gratefully onto the plush seat. Not until he got behind the wheel and turned the key, did she stop to think it was a risk she was taking. As her fear of the dog receded, a new worry took its place. She kept her hand on the door latch.

Interpreting her anxious glance on the mark, he murmured, "A little late to be getting cautious, isn't it?"

"You seemed the lesser of two evils," she blurted.

He threw back his head and laughed. "If there's a compliment in there, it's pretty well concealed." While she blushed anew, he asked her address, then drove the car into light morning traffic.

The only softening of a decidedly masculine profile was a thick dark fringe of lashes hooding grey eyes. His jawline was hard and distinct, his cheekbone arched high and ruggedly hewn. Yet for all his look of toughness, she saw nothing dark or sinister in his face. Relaxing her hold on the door latch, she murmured, "You thought it was silly of me, being afraid of that dog."

He did not deny it; he didn't reply at all.

Hoping he wasn't thinking too badly of her, Mandy wished she could justify her behavior in his eyes. Knowing she couldn't, she murmured an inadequate,

"Sometimes, when a person is afraid of a dog, the dog senses it."

"That's true," he agreed.

"And even if the dog isn't ordinarily aggressive," she struggled on, "he may become that way, thinking he has the upper hand."

He raised a questioning eyebrow. "You've had a bad experience or two with dogs?"

"Only one. Since that time, I've been careful." Warding off ugly memories, she added, "Thank you for being so understanding."

"Glad I could help." He stopped the car in front of her apartment building. "This is the place, isn't it?"

Mandy nodded. She shifted the sack of dry cat food and her pocketbook into a comfortable carrying position.

A twinkle lit his eye. "I take it you haven't had any bad moments with cats."

Thrown off guard by his sudden grin, Mandy went blank for a second before realizing he meant the cat food. "Oh, that. It isn't mine. I don't have a cat either. Though I'm not afraid of them. I've just never gotten around to acquiring one.

"Of course," she continue, "there's my neighbor's cat, Willie. He thinks he belongs to the entire apartment population. Occasionally he scratches at my door and I let him in. And as long as he's not in the mood to de-leaf my plants, he's welcome to stay until he becomes bored."

He grinned like he found her sudden talkative spell a welcome change, and Mandy stopped short. Why ever was she rambling on like a star-struck teen? She hadn't run that many words together since the time she tried to explain to her father how she had put the car in the ditch, fighting off one invading bumblebee. And that had been years ago!

"Thank you again for the rescue." She climbed hurriedly out of the car. "And the ride home too, Mr . . ." she paused, confused all over again.

12

"Cooke." His grin widened. "T.K. Cooke."

"Mr. Cooke," Mandy finished, and closed the car door behind her.

He waved and pulled back into traffic. Mandy went inside, half disappointed he hadn't asked her her name.

However, once she had delivered the cat food, Mandy returned to her sewing and forgot all about the man, if not the dog. It seemed she had been sewing only a short time when the doorbell rang.

"Fudge," she muttered, pushing back her chair.

An owl-eyed little girl took a step back and whispered up at her, "Would you like to buy a box of Girlscout cookies?"

The poor child looked so nervous, Mandy bought two boxes just to coax a smile. It seemed she had no more than resumed her work at the machine when Gram called.

"It's hard to believe Ellen is old enough to marry," Gram launched into what had all the makings for a long, long conversation.

"She's twenty-two, Gram," Mandy reminded, wise to the fact Gram was subtly hinting that *she,* Ellen's senior by two years, ought to be thinking of marriage herself.

"I know that, dear. And I suppose marriage will be wonderful for her. She can be so flighty!"

Accustomed to Gram's theory every good woman needed a good man to love, to cherish, and yes, to obey, Mandy pulled the ironing board nearer the phone and used it as a work table while Gram ran on.

"Yes, Gram," she would say every now and then.

"By the way, how is that young man of yours?" Gram finally stopped beating around the bush.

"Corey's just fine, Gram, but he isn't *my* young man. We're just friends." Putting the last pin in a side-seam, Mandy tried to find a new subject. "Is Ellen coming here later?"

"Yes, she's stopping by to see how the brides-maids' dresses are coming," Gram said with marked boredom, then back-tracked, "Why haven't you brought Corey to dinner recently?"

"He's pretty busy with that company of his. Four Seasons Pet Supply Manufacturing is a booming business." Mandy looked longingly at her out-of-reach machine, than at the clock. Gram had talked fifteen minutes and was just warming up. The filmy fabric of bridesmaids' dress number one draped the ironing board in silent accusation. How was she ever to get her work done?

"Why don't you invite Corey to church Sunday?" Gram chimed out her suggestion as if it just had occurred to her. "The two of you could come to Sunday dinner here afterward. We're having chicken."

"Corey doesn't show much interest in church," Mandy said in truth. "I don't want to push."

"An invite isn't a push. Sometimes you have to put feet on your prayers," Gram said, and Mandy wondered how she knew she had been praying for Corey. But as she talked on, a noose of desperation tightened. Ellen's wedding was June twenty-seventh, one month, ten days. This was the first of the bridesmaid dresses, and Ellen's bridal gown was still a long, solid piece of fabric waiting to be cut. Likewise with the flower-girl's dress. And Gram hadn't even decided on pattern *or* fabric yet.

Standing there, impatiently twisting the phone cord around one finger as she considered the upcoming wedding as well as her regular orders, Mandy had good cause to feel tense over the shortness of time and the irritation of unnecessary interruptions. Today, between the doorbell, the phone, and the tricky electrical short in her machine cord, she was near the point of panic.

Gram finally let her go, but the two phone calls that

followed and a ringing doorbell drove her over the brink. After refusing the vacuum cleaner salesman's offer of a free demonstration vacuuming of her apartment, Mandy took the phone off the hook and tacked a note to her apartment door:

"Seamstress seaming. Please do not disturb."

Not very tactful, perhaps, but Ellen would never forgive her if she had to glide to the altar in her petticoat. The interruptions stopped, but worry had robbed Mandy of the enjoyment of the project.

Early in the afternoon, she lifted her head at the sound of giggles in the hallway. The sign, however, proved effective. The giggles died away and whoever it was left her in peace. Several hours passed. Mandy began listening for Ellen to pop in, knowing the note wouldn't intimidate her sister for a second.

It didn't either. Not bothering with the bell, Ellen used her own key and sailed in wanting to know, "How many dresses did you finish today?"

Mandy tried to quell her with a lofty glance. "I'm still working on the first."

"You're kidding!" Ellen's face fell. "I thought you'd have two done at least. You're generally so nimble-fingered." Mandy bit back a cranky retort and several dozen excuses, but something in her expression must have gotten through to Ellen, for she rushed on, apologetic, almost.

"It is an intricate pattern, of course. And I wouldn't trust anyone but you to do it. Oh, Mand, I simply can't wait! Isn't it going to be a gorgeous wedding?"

Watching her sister, her lovely hands caressing the ivory fabric, her slender body poised like a bird about to take flight, Mandy found herself thinking every hectic moment she had endured was going to be worth it. Ellen had always been vivacious and radiant, but now, even more so. It must be a wonderful thing to be so gloriously head over heels in love!

"You look as if you've just swallowed a rainbow,

pot of gold and all." Mandy touched her sister's hand. "Is it really that good, Ellie?"

Ellen trickled laughter and gave Mandy a hug. "It's better! Someday, you'll know, Mand. Really you will. And then you'll forgive me for driving you so crazy, wanting everything about this wedding to be as perfect as my life with Gregory is going to be!"

Mandy's face fell into thoughtful lines as, in silence, she prayed Ellen was right. Ellen grabbed her again, and hugged her harder.

"Don't look so serious. I'm getting married, not drafted!"

Freeing Mandy as abruptly as she had grabbed her, Ellen did a little dance around the room, pausing to straighten a framed picture here, a kitchen-chair cushion there, and all the while, talking of Gregory and their wedding.

Watching her, Mandy thought of her father. He might be a history teacher, dusty in the eyes of his students, but to her, he had the insight of a poet and the words to match.

A long stem yellow rose. That was what he called Ellen. Tall, graceful, fair-skinned, silvery blond and dewey-eyed, Ellen wore the description well.

The only feature she and Ellen shared was the Holt face—heart-shaped and delicate. But, Mandy asked in her soul, who noticed a heart-shaped face on a little brown wood nut? That was what her father likened *her* to, not only because her eyes and hair were soft brown, with the hint of red of an acorn, but also because of her love of the Ozark hills and woodlands.

"Gregory's mother is having a few friends in for dinner this evening." Ellen jerked her out of her thoughts. "You're invited. That is, if you can spare time from the dresses."

"Thank her, but no. On top of my other work, Kay called from the dance studio today. She wants a dozen butterfly costumes for the children's fall recital."

"Pooh! That's months yet."

Well aware Ellen didn't understand the pressure she felt over deadlines, Mandy let it go. "It will roll around, though. As will Claire Manson's ocean cruise, and I've scarcely started her wardrobe."

"Her again?" Ellen screwed up her soft mouth.

Mandy chuckled. "You should see the outfits she wants made!"

"Colorful?" Ellen ventured a guess.

"To say the least."

Ellen sighed dramatically. "I wish Gregory could get a month off for our honeymoon. An ocean cruise, just imagine! Wouldn't that be something? But alas, I guess a week in St. Louis will have to do."

"Poor thing, you," Mandy mocked sympathy, for though Ellen yearned to travel, Mandy found it hard to understand why anyone would believe there could be anything lovelier than the Missouri hill country surrounding their town of Stratton.

Ellen eventually left as she had come—in a scurry—and Mandy settled down to her sewing again. Luck was not with her. The front door vibrated with a loud knocking.

Mandy shoved her chair back and plodded to the door, wondering why Corey persistently refused to use the doorbell. Perhaps he liked to hear his knuckles pounding wood.

Corey stepped in from the corridor, a take-out pizza in one hand, her note in the other.

"This is *not* a very friendly note," he said, waving it under her nose.

"But effective to a point," she parried words with him. "Only you and Ellen have dared barge past it."

That distinction earned her a broad smile. Perhaps it was his size that made assertiveness important to Corey. Though often enough he had told her that when a guy feels ten feet tall, five feet seven inches will do.

17

"I'd have settled for 'Come on in,'" he remarked, though not the least insulted by her blank look. He walked his feisty strut past her into the kitchen where, by random search, he located a pizza pan.

"I'm working here," Mandy protested, and indicated the cluttered kitchen table as he proceeded to pop the pizza into the oven for reheating.

"But you still have to eat." He made a logical assumption.

"*When* I get hungry."

"Don't be inhospitable, Mandy. I'm saving you the trouble of fixing a meal. Where are your plates?"

Mandy released an exasperated sigh. "Corey, this has been a terrible day. I've so much to do."

"Poor Mand," he sympathized. "Perhaps I can cheer you up. Do you want to get the plates or shall I? I know, you get them, I'll clear the table."

"Don't you dare touch that dress!" Mandy yelped. "You just licked your fingers. I saw you!"

Corey gave her a cheeky grin. "You'd better clear it then. And, I might add, your note was accurate. You *are* steaming."

"Not steaming, *seaming*."

Corey shoved the note under her nose and in spite of her efforts, a grin tugged at her lips. The letter "t" had been squeezed into the word "seaming" and colorful heat-waves squiggled all over the note.

"It must have been the Murphy girls. I heard giggles at my door this afternoon." Giving up on getting rid of him, Mandy started clearing the table.

"Young delinquents," Corey said flippantly. "Why weren't they in school?"

"This is Saturday, Corey." Mandy rolled her eyes heavenward. "I don't know about you. You'd better ease up on the work a bit, the way you keep losing track of the days."

Corey spilled out a long-suffering groan. "Thomas pushes, you know. Work, work, work."

By "Thomas," he could mean his secretary, whom he affectionately called Thomas, or it could be his silent partner in the pet supply company, Thomas . . . Mandy tried to trigger the name by word association but it wouldn't come.

Not that it was important. She didn't know Corey's partner, nor did she *have* to know him to realize Corey's own ambition was the driving force behind him. He dreamed big dreams and they seemed to pay off. Four Seasons Pet Supply was doing marvelously well.

Thomas . . . again she tried to recall the last name. A very common name, it seemed, but elusive. Anyway, the man was an ex-army buddy of Corey's, and something of a recluse. Or so Corey had told her the only time she had voiced any curiosity about the man.

Before the pet supply manufacturing company, Corey had by his own admission, been a used car salesman. Perhaps, Mandy thought sometime later as they polished off the pizza, that was where he had mastered the art of persuasion. She could feature him talking a shaky little old lady with short legs into buying a four-wheel drive pick-up truck with about as much ease as he had just talked her into running across town to tour the new executive offices at the plant.

At the door of the factory, Corey waved the nightwatchman aside, saying, "I'm going to give Miss Holt a tour of the building. Don't let us keep you. I'll lock up as we leave, you can be sure."

Mandy followed Corey through the heart of the factory and up a flight of carpeted stairs. Corey held open an office door designated, "Miss Thomas." There was the scent of newness about the office, fresh paint, plush brown carpet, modern furnishings.

"Nice," Mandy murmured, running her hand along the desk-top. "Very nice."

She followed Corey into his adjoining office. A

massive desk occupied the center of the room. Shelves of books lined the walls. Mandy picked out a title at random—*Pet Lovers Unite*. She chuckled, for as ironic as it seemed, Corey didn't like animals.

"Do you really read these books?"

He grinned, unabashed. "No. But they lend atmosphere, don't you think?"

Without awaiting her reply, he fumbled with a switch and revealed a hidden panel. "There is even piped in music, if I can just find the right button."

Simultaneously, a loud blast of music and the ringing of the phone assaulted their ears. Frantically turning knobs to find the volume control, Corey shouted, "Get the phone, will you Mand?"

She did, though the voice in her ear was hard to hear thanks to the ear-splitting volume of the music. To the best of her ability, she interpreted the words as:

"Thank goodness I got you and not that awful answering machine. Tell Corey I got his message about the flea collars. And yes, I agree an adjustment on the assembly line should be made as quickly as possible.

"I'm flying to Chicago for a meeting with a new distributor, as planned, so Corey can handle it alone. After Chicago, I'll follow the usual circuit. Barring no emergencies, I should return to Stratton in three weeks, four at the most.

"Oh, and Miss Thomas? Have I mislayed my copy of *Wilderness Bay* at the office? I can't seem to find it here at home."

At the precise moment Mandy began to explain she wasn't Miss Thomas, Corey cut off the music and she was, to her chagrin, all but shouting into the phone.

"Excuse me." A rush of color crept up her collar. "I didn't mean to shout. Corey was showing me his office and how the piped in music works. It works very loudly, I'm afraid," she rambled on, unable to find a clear path out, and equally unable to just be still. "But it seems to be under control now. Anyway, I was trying to say, I'm not Miss Thomas. Here, why don't you just talk to Corey?"

Mandy shoved the phone into Corey's waiting hand. Corey's conversation with the man she assumed to be his partner ran on and on. Something of a bookworm when time allowed, Mandy surveyed the shelves with interest.

The title, *Wilderness Bay* seemed to leap out at her. She took it from the shelf, handling it with care, for it was dog-earred and worn.

"Tell him the book is here," she whispered into Corey's unoccupied ear.

"Thomas? Just a second. Mandy's found your book. Yes, on the shelves. Of course I'll hang onto it. I haven't turned this office into a lending library yet."

Corey laughed then, as if the remark had earned an indignant response.

"How did you get his book?" Mandy asked when Corey's conversation ended. "I thought he never came to the office. That *was* your mysterious silent partner, wasn't it?"

Corey fingered the book without looking at her. "He stops by from time to time," came his vague reply.

"Hmm. And here I thought the man was a recluse."

"Thomas does like his privacy. Not to mention that he finds offices confining." Corey held the door for her. "Shall we go?"

Because he was seldom moody, Mandy had difficulty understanding Corey's sudden taciturn attitude. The drive home was a quiet one, bringing strangely to mind Gram's breezy, "Invite him to church."

More and more of late, Mandy found herself praying for Corey. His disinterest in God was a burden on her heart, though she would never find the words to tell him so anymore than she could walk up to a stranger and ask, "Do you know Christ as your Savior?" Her service unto the Lord was done in a quiet way—making choir robes, cleaning the church, helping out in the nursery. Words came hard to her. She wished the burden would go away.

CHAPTER 2

ON THEIR RETURN TO Mandy's apartment building, they ran head-on into Claire Manson rapping at Mandy's door.

"Oh, I'm so glad I didn't miss you!" The young widow lay a diamond-sparkling hand on Mandy's arm. "I was about to leave a note for you to call. Mandy, I've found the most darling swim suit pattern. You *will* do it for me, won't you? You know how much trouble I have getting a store-bought suit to fit me properly."

So saying, she plucked the swimsuit pattern and slick Hawaiian print fabric from a sack. "I just couldn't resist. It's definitely my color, don't you agree?"

She flicked at Corey with a flirting, expectant expression, and wearing a smile like a banner of admiration, Corey agreed, "I'll go along with that. It's your color, all right."

Claire gave a throaty laugh. "Isn't he sweet? Where'd you find *him*, Mandy?"

"At Pet World," Corey jumped in and answered.

"She was window shopping for Ida Princeton's cat, Willie. I kept her from buying the wrong brand trinket."

Claire's smile was puzzled, provocative and meant soley for Corey. Yet it was Mandy who made introductions and explained she had met Corey by chance. He had been representing Four Seasons Pet Supply products, introducing their line to the store manager at Pet World. Throughout her recital, Corey and Mrs. Manson exchanged looks, *long* looks, of mutual admiration.

Claire did, though, manage to get down to business eventually—the business of convincing Mandy she certainly had time before August to add this one more very small garment to her list of projects.

Small—she had that part right, at least. Time? She was wrong there, but she was also the type who couldn't take "no" for an answer, and continued to hound until Mandy said she would try, just to get rid of the woman.

Mandy unlocked her door, feeling the pressure mounting. She disliked being shouldered into taking on more than she could comfortably arrange to complete.

"You should have left the note on my door," Mandy grumbled to Corey, who followed her in. "How am I ever going to get all my sewing completed in time if people keep calling and stopping by to coax me into taking on more and more work?"

Corey closed the door with his foot and caught Mandy's face between his two hands. "Why don't you give up this silly seamstress business, Mandy?"

Knowing what was coming, she tried to forestall it with a little laugh. "Because I like eating."

"You could marry me. I've asked you often enough, haven't I?"

About once a month, for the last six months, but who was counting? Mandy freed herself. "I *like* my sewing, Corey. And I *like* my independence just as much as you like yours. Marriage isn't at all what I need or want. What I *need* is a few peaceful uninterrupted days to do my work. Say three weeks on an uninhabited island."

Corey took her refusal in cheerful stride. "There aren't any deserted islands in Missouri. None that I know of, anyway."

"I'm serious!" Mandy insisted, feeling very weary. "I really wish I had a secret place. A place where no one would call or interrupt my work. People think because I'm home, I'm available!

"Gram calls and talks as if I have all the time in the world. Ellen pops in, looks wide-eyed and asks, 'Is that *all* you have done?', then turns right around in the next breath and invites me to Gregory's for dinner and then you . . ."

"Okay, okay," Corey interrupted, trying not to chuckle at her sudden outburst of frustration. "I get your message. I was leaving anyway."

He kissed her in parting, a kiss she accepted out of habit. Sometimes, she thought as she closed the door behind him, it seemed that habit was the main ingredient which bound her to Corey. In the beginning, she had wondered if love might grow out of their relationship, but it hadn't. Not for her, at least.

Perhaps not even for Corey. Sure, he asked her to marry him, but lightly, almost as if he anticipated her response and was satisfied with things as they stood. Far from convinced was she, that any one woman was the love of Corey's life. He seemed to adore all women. If she ever said, "Yes, let's do get married," it would probably scare him right into the next century.

Uncharacteristically out of sorts, Mandy returned to her sewing. The evening sun had set, her eyes were tired and the light over the table seemed insufficient for the task of fitting a lace bodice inset into the yellow taffeta gown. After an hour, she put the case on her portable machine, bathed, and called it a day.

Too tired even to set her alarm, Mandy collapsed into bed. Yet sleep was slow to claim her. The muffled sounds of neighboring apartment dwellers settling down for the night weren't the problem. The problem was within her.

The same loss of peace, the irrational upset over the dog, and the irritability which had marred her day now haunted her conscience. Generally happy to run small errands for Miss Princeton, she had done it today out of a disgruntled sense of duty. And she had complained not only to herself, but to Corey about Gram's phone call. Gram! Whom did she love any better?

What was wrong with her, anyway? She had her family, her health, an occupation she enjoyed. Why was she feeling so dissatisfied?

Unable, though she was, to put her finger on *why* her day had gone wrong, Mandy was certain of the source of renewed energy and enthusiasm. Eyes closed, heart open to God, she prayed.

Mandy had just stepped in from church the next day when Corey phoned.

"Have I got a surprise for you!" his voice rang of self-congratulations. "I've found your deserted island, so to speak!"

Mandy hooked the toe of her shoe around a kitchen chair, pulled it closer and sat down. "And all I need is transportation, is that it? Like an airline ticket to the South Pacific?"

"I'm serious," he said, sounding so. "I really have found a place where you can work undisturbed for a couple of weeks. It's only fifteen miles out of town. Plenty close enough to drive back and forth every day. And the best part is, the place is secluded. There isn't even a phone. You'll have peace and quiet oozing out your ears."

Alive with interest, Mandy voiced a cautious, "You're not teasing me, are you? You really know of such a paradise?"

"Yes, and I can't imagine why I didn't think of it yesterday, it's such a grand idea. You see, Tommy and I bought this piece of property recently. Tommy was interested because it borders land . . ."

"You are serious! Corey, how can I ever thank you? You've saved my sanity!"

He laughed, pleased with her reaction. "I've only seen the place once. It's mostly hills and timber, though there's a creek and a small glade, too. Anyway, on the bank of the creek, there is a sportsman's lodge. Mind you, it isn't a fancy building. But I think it's suitable for your needs."

"It sounds marvelous. I'll take it sight unseen. What's the rent?"

"Mandy!" Corey exclaimed in a hurt tone. "Who said anything about rent? I'm lending you the use of the lodge for two or three weeks, long enough for you to catch up on your sewing. Would you like to drive out this afternoon and take a look?"

Would she like it? It was an answer to prayer! After changing into white slacks and a soft blue blouse, Mandy went down to the lobby to watch for Corey. When his red sports car pulled up to the curb, she sprang out the door.

"This is really sweet of you, Corey," she said on the ride out of the city. "And I was such a cross bear yesterday. I didn't mean to be. It was just all the pressure of getting my jobs completed on time got to me."

Corey cracked a wide grin. "So long as you're sweetness and light today. Yesterday's dead and gone."

His philosophy on life? Mandy wasn't fooled into believing it. There was a hidden depth to Corey, things in his past he chose not to speak of, dreams in his future he did not disclose.

Studying his profile, she wondered why nothing there ever caught at her heart and sent it racing. It was a handsome profile, marked by high cheekbones and a distinguished Roman nose. Yet to her, it remained the face of a dear friend. Love took time, so her father said. Enduring love, a lifetime of testing.

The shadowy remains of yesterday's melancholy threatened to settle, but Mandy shook it off and concentrated on the passing countryside.

The two lane highway was familiar. It wove a path between towering limestone bluffs, crossed and re-crossed a meandering creek, and skirted hills handing out hair-pin turns and s-curves like a crooked dealer.

She rolled her window down and let the wind whip her hair back from her face. The air smelled clean and fresh, intoxicating. The breeze seemed to carry away her worries about her work and Ellen's wedding, even nagging wonderings about her relationship with Corey.

How she loved the hills and nestled hollows! There was an agelessness about the Ozark country that intrigued her. The stony cliffs sat like sentinels, hinting of secrets possessed, wisdom earned and knowledge to impart if a weary soul would but take the time to walk the quiet pathways to the bluffs.

The fragrant scent of dogwoods was on the open air while redbuds in full bloom made a splash of color against greening hillsides. A sigh of pure contentment escaped her lips.

Corey paid her a lazy smile. "I think you're a country girl at heart."

"Perhaps. I lived in the country when I was very small. But after my mother died, we moved to town. I've always regretted that myself, though it put Dad closer to his work. And Ellen probably would have gone stir crazy in the country. Gram seems well suited to town also."

"You're the only misfit in the bunch, huh?"

"I don't know. I'm not too sure about Dad. He's always enjoyed long walks in the hills."

Corey made a turn onto a road that appeared seldom traveled. Whiskers of grass poked up through the gravel. A mile further on, he turned again, this time onto a dirt track. It hadn't seen much recent traffic, judging by the manner in which beech trees, oaks and maples encroached.

A crude but sturdy wooden bridge took them across a rippling creek and there hugging a hill, was the sportsman's lodge. The rectangular building was constructed of native lumber. On one end, a stone chimney rose from the ground. Ivy was beginning to creep up it, giving the building the impression of belonging to the surrounding hills and woodlands.

Corey located a door key under the welcome mat. Inside, the afternoon sun filtered through red-checked curtains, making sunbeam patches on the dusty floor tiles. Corey's footsteps echoed through the sparsely furnished building as he searched out the electrical box and turned on the main switch.

"I warned you it wasn't fancy," he said, joining her at the door. "What do you think?"

She liked the casual, outdoorsy atmosphere and was quick to assure him as she began a tour of the place. Corey watched with undisguised amusement as she poked around in the kitchenette, checked out the small bathroom, and finally, crossed to the far end of the building to stand before the huge stone fireplace.

From the kitchenette end of the building, Corey cupped his hand to his mouth. "Hello down there! Are you still here?"

Mandy giggled at his antics. "All this empty space is a little overwhelming."

"And not the least cozy."

"Coziness, I think, is a state of mind," Mandy mused. "Anyway, I don't care. It's a place off by myself. I'll be able to work undisturbed."

"That, you can count on." Corey dragged a couple of mismatched chairs up to the fireplace, gave them a lick and a promise dusting with his handkerchief and waited for her to sit before dropping down himself.

"There is one hitch," he said. "You'll need to get your back-log of work caught up in two, three weeks at the most."

"I haven't even settled in and you're giving me my eviction notice?"

Disconcerted, Corey took great care in refolding his handkerchief. "As I told you, the building belongs to Tommy, too. He has some tentative plans for using it around the second weekend in June. So if you could be out of here a few days before that . . ."

"Of course, Corey," Mandy rushed in, ashamed she had sounded unappreciative. "And you don't have to apologize. It's very sweet of you and Thomas to let me use it at all."

His evasive, "No problem," stirred a doubt in her.

"Your partner *does* know, doesn't he? That I'll be using the lodge?"

"Well, I couldn't get him on the phone this morning," Corey hedged. "But I'll call him later. Anyway, I'm certain he won't mind."

Frowning, she brushed a tendril of hair back from her face. "Maybe I shouldn't make any plans until you've talked it over with him."

"Nonsense. Tommy won't care." Corey got to his feet, and reaching for her hand, pulled her up too. "At any rate, the building is half mine, remember."

"Which half?" Mandy was still not entirely convinced she should move her sewing things in without at least a word of consent from Corey's partner.

"Which half do you like best?" A roguish grin darted across his face. "Whichever, you're welcome to it. Stop worrying about Tommy. Let's go back to town for a bite of dinner. I'm starved."

Wistfully, Mandy murmured, "If only I'd thought

to pack a picnic lunch. What a perfect spot to spend the afternoon. So quiet and peaceful.''

Taking her hand in his, Corey lead the way back to the car. "A couple days of this quiet and you'll be yearning for the hustle and bustle of city traffic.''

She gave him an impish smile. "I'm commuting, remember? I'll get a good dose of road hogs and horn-honkers every day, so you needn't worry about me missing a thing!''

Though Mandy had asked him to, Corey didn't call that evening to assure her he had spoken to Thomas and gotten his permission for her to use the lodge for two or three weeks. And, because she awoke to leave a full hour before daylight, she couldn't call him the next morning.

As she packed sewing supplies, the makings of the second bridesmaid's dress, a hearty sack lunch and a hoard of cleaning supplies into her car, she found herself recalling her own brief conversation with Corey's partner, Thomas. Why, he had said he was leaving for Chicago today. Which meant, even if Corey hadn't managed to get in touch with him, he wasn't going to be around to object to her setting up shop in the lodge.

Her worry gone on a wave of relief, she continued to pack, then paused again, another thought occurring. Odd, Corey saying Thomas had plans for the lodge over the second weekend in June, when Thomas had said himself in that mixed-up conversation, he would be gone three or four weeks. He might not even be back by the second weekend in June.

She shrugged. Maybe that's why his plans were tentative. It was nothing to her anyway. She had Corey's permission, a door key and a head packed full of plans.

A pale dawn pink was stealing darkness from the sky by degrees as Mandy started on her way. She maneuvered the twisting, turning country road with careful attention and even then, almost missed the unobstrusive turn-off.

The dirt track was even harder to find, though once on it, she recognized familiar land marks. The small bridge was a welcome sight and just beyond it, the lodge.

Knowing she didn't dare take her fabric into the lodge until the place had been cleaned, Mandy unloaded her cleaning supplies. Once inside, she pulled down the faded curtains and flung the windows open. Her broom swished over window sills and floors, then paused from time to time as she listened to the warbling chorus of birds just outside her door.

Mopping the floor proved a bigger task than she had anticipated. Her third bucket of mop water had turned a dingy grey before the dull red tile gleamed to her satisfaction.

Wanting to give the floor adequate time to dry before walking across it again, Mandy emptied the last bucket of water, upended the bucket and sat down.

She wiped her hands down the sides of her jeans and retied the kerchief that held her hair back from her face. The sun was warm and relaxing, though the morning was still young.

Off in the distance, she recognized the bay of a hound, but thought little of it, the sound was so far away. She stretched her arms overhead, appreciating the gorgeous day. A cloudless blue sky stretched beyond a criss-cross of tree branches. Fragile wildflowers dotted the hillside in gentle colors and the winding creek played a trickling song.

She walked a ways from the lodge and leaned against the bole of a huge red oak. A rabbit scurried her way, panicked at her unexpected presence and circled the tree before zig-zagging up the hill.

Chuckling, Mandy wandered up the hillside too. The branches of the same red oak she had leaned against at the bottom of the hill stretched so wide she could with but a little effort reach out and touch them.

Suddenly, a sound, much closer now, jerked her out of her lethargic mood. The baying sounded not like one dog, but several. She squinted into the brilliance of the morning sun, peering down toward the lodge.

Just approaching it were three yapping beagles. Her nerves seemed to shatter like glass as the dogs splashed across the creek, scrambled up the bank, and mouths frothy with the thrill of chase, skirted the lodge.

For a spot in time, she stood frozen, watching them tear around the base of the oak some forty feet down. But as they tore up the hillside toward her, she shook off her terror and looked for a place of refuge. Other than the one oak tree, the hillside was bare of shelter.

Ever closer the dogs came, a high excited bark splitting the air, as, noses to the ground, they came on, filling her with renewed panic. She started to run, then cried out in pain as a small whispy branch of the towering oak caught in her hair.

The lead dog was only yards away. She darted a frantic glance at the wide-spread upper branch of the oak. Terror masked as cold reason insisted, "Go for it! Jump!"

Perhaps to an agile lad, it wouldn't have looked like such a chance, leaping for a solid piece of that out-stretched branch. But there wasn't a scrap of tomboy in her and the branch seemed like a reckless chance.

No more so than the dogs. Bending her knees, she sprang forward, stretched her arms so far overhead the muscles jerked as her hands made contact with the rough bark of the tree. She made it! Getting a better hold, she flailed her legs like scissors and finally hooked one over the branch.

Below, the dogs were raising a terrible din. She pulled herself up to straddle the branch just as they flew beneath her. Two continued up the hill at a dead run, but the third trotted to a stop, threw a brown gaze upward and gave a sharp bark.

Heart pounding like a war drum, Mandy whispered, "Go away, please just go away!"

The dog cocked his satiny head, his liquid brown eyes melting away at her terror, leaving her simply frightened and more than a little foolish-feeling. The dogs had been after the rabbit, not her.

"Go on, doggie. Find your pals," she urged him.

The dog wagged his tail and with an answering yip, dropped down on the slant of the hill. Tail wagging counted for naught where Mandy was concerned. Dogs weren't to be trusted, be they toy poodles, great danes or anything in between.

Her helplessness was familiar. She clung to the tree, logic telling her the dog meant no harm, old lingering fears stubbornly insisting she exercise extreme caution, take no chances, wait the dog out.

Dear God, I need help! Help, help, help! The word echoed over and over in her head, outshouted only by the loud rush in her ears and the rapid beat of her heart.

Below, the dog yip-yip-yipped, but Mandy didn't open her eyes until she heard the scurry of his feet taking him away. Thank you, Lord!

Mandy looked up the hill. The dog was nowhere in sight. She cast a glance in the downward direction, and was hampered by thick foliage. She pushed the leaves aside, then gasped as, from an upturned face, smoky grey eyes peered back at her. Incredible as it seemed, it was the man from the supermarket. The very same man who had rescued her from the German shepherd.

"You!" Heat-waves flooded her face as shock wrung the word from her.

The inscrutable eyes began to twinkle. "Just look what you've treed, old boy. And just this morning, I accused you of being the world's worst hunter." He stooped to fondle the dog's velvety ears.

A dark frown hovered about her sensitive mouth. "That isn't funny."

The man hid a grin and stroked the wagging dog's freckled chest. When his mouth was straight again, he spoke up into the tree. "You might as well come down. Clancy doesn't bite. Not big game, anyway."

Ignoring his last comment, Mandy said stiffly, "Just the same . . ."

Amusement danced in his watchful eyes. "You'd like me to get rid of him?"

Mute with humiliation, she nodded.

"Very well." The man turned full attention on the dog, gave him a final petting, then pointed back in the direction of the lodge. "To the truck, boy. Go on."

Without much more than a backward glance, the dog trotted off down the hill. Grudgingly, Mandy said, "He at least is trained."

"All my dogs are," he dismissed the subject. "Now, why don't you get down before a sparrow makes a nest in your hair? Careful, I'll help you," he cautioned, seemingly enjoying his repeat performance of deliverer of a lady in distress.

Pride prickled. "I can manage, thank you."

He backed off a step and poked his finger-tips into the pockets of his comfortably faded jeans. Trying not to notice he looked as well-suited to them as he had to his business suit, Mandy wriggled around until her feet dangled a few feet off the ground, then hesitated to make the final leap.

The slant of the hill seemed steeper than she'd noticed upon climbing it. Though her arms began to ache, she was hesitant to let go of the branch. If she didn't get her footing right, she'd probably tumble, perhaps all the way to the bottom of the hill. That ought to be the capper on total humiliation.

"Let go," the man said. "If you start to fall, I'll catch you."

Spouting independence from her precarious position seemed fool-hardy. Despite her longing to tell him to go about his own business and leave her to hers, she gave a nod, then jumped. As her feet connected with the ground, she began to slide in the dew-kissed grass.

Strong arms, the muscles pronounced, reached out to steady her. Skin tingling at his touch, Mandy delivered a formal, "Thank you, I'm fine now Mr. Cooke."

"T.K. Remember?" He stepped away from her, finger-tips hooking his pockets again.

Sensitive to his probing gaze, Mandy averted her face. "T.K. then."

A smile spread across his rough hewn features. "That's better. If I'm going to keep rescuing you from the canines of Shane County, we should at least be on a first name basis, don't you agree, Miss . . . ?"

Feeling prickly all over again, Mandy ignored his bid for a name. Tilting her chin, she clipped out, "If people didn't let their dogs roam free, I wouldn't be in need of rescuing. There is such a thing as a leash law, I believe."

Mastering the amusement in his voice, he returned mildly, "Out here? I hardly think so."

"If you don't mind my asking, what are you doing out here anyway?" Mandy said, riled by his superior manner. "This *is* private property."

He arched a dark eyebrow. "Indeed? That being the case, maybe I should ask you the same question. What are you doing here, besides climbing trees?"

Forcibly relaxing her hands from tightened fists, Mandy used her haughtiest tone. "The use of the lodge is mine by the permission of the owner."

"Is that so?"

"Yes, that's so."

"And who might that be?"

"Corey Stapleton. Perhaps you've heard of him." Noting with satisfaction a glint of recognition darken his eye, she added, "He owns Four Seasons Pet Supply Manufacturing. That is, he and a Thomas

Something-Or-The-Other do. I've misplaced his last name."

"I see." Casting a look over his shoulder and up the hill they'd just descended, the man muttered, "A matter of minor importance, I gather."

Then, without warning, he whistled an ear-splitting whistle. Seeing her wince, he apologized.

"I'm sorry, I should have warned you. There are two more dogs."

"I know. I saw them." Apprehension shrinking her irritation with him, she asked, "They come when you whistle?"

"Most of the time. Unless they feel they've been cheated out of their fair amount of exercise. In which case, like disobedient children, they dally along until I have to go after them."

Fervently hoping the dogs were in a dallying mood, Mandy backtracked to their previous topic of conversation. "Were you aware the sportsman's lodge had been sold?"

"Yes." He kept walking.

"Then you have Corey's permission to exercise your dogs here?" she followed, needled by his economy of words.

"You might say that."

Under the circumstance, the dry look he spared her was disconcerting. Almost intimidating. Mandy walked beside him in silence a moment. She stole a glance or two at his face finding something there that, oddly enough, made her think of Corey.

Why, she couldn't fathom. He was tall, Corey was not. He was dark of complexion, Corey was fair. He was grey-eyed, Corey blue. Perhaps it was something about his facial structure. The high cheek bones. On Corey they were less pronounced, interestingly attractive.

On this man, they lent an inscrutable signature of character: not readily swayed or hoodwinked, she ventured, and seldom if ever bested. Looking at him, she envisioned somewhere in his family tree a regal warrior, proud and militant.

"You have just three dogs?" she questioned, for want of a better topic.

He whistled again, looked up the hill and took his time answering. "My grandfather and I raise beagles."

Involuntarily, she shuddered. "Never mind, don't tell me how many you have. All I want to know is, are you in the habit of running your dogs here?"

"Not always, but sometimes. And never all at the same time."

As if that was supposed to calm her fears! The thought of encountering any of them, alone or in mass force was unsettling enough to turn this valley of Eden into a shadowy place. From now on, she'd be less easy about stepping foot out of the lodge.

"Is this the time of day you generally exercise them?" she tried to pin-point an hour of safety.

A flicker of annoyance crossed his face. "Look, there's no way I can set up a time table, if that's what you're asking. I'm going to be gone for a few weeks and my grandfather will be exercising the dogs. As the spirit moves him," he added with meaning. "He isn't a man to let his life be ruled by a clock."

"So what you're saying is, I'll just have to take my chances."

"Yes, that's pretty much what I'm saying, since you refuse to believe the dogs are harmless, Miss . . ."

"Holt, Amanda Holt," she gave her name on a spurt of impatience. "Perhaps if I were to speak to Corey about these dogs of yours, he could suggest a solution."

"Do that. His reply should be interesting." Again, that enigmatic flicker in his eyes.

"I will. He shares my aversion to dogs, you know. Not that he's afraid. He just doesn't like them."

"Or any other animal," the man said.

Mandy shot him a veiled glance. "You really *do* know Corey, don't you."

"I said that I did. Were you doubting me?"

Mandy admitted it with a careless shrug.

His mouth quirked. "You aren't a very trusting soul, are you? First dogs, now me."

Something in his tone made her ashamed. She said, "I suppose to a man who raises dogs, my fear of them seems pretty silly."

"Not your fear of the German shepherd," he said, trying, she assumed, to be neutral. "They have a reputation for being unpredictable. There is something wild and wonderful in them, but it isn't a good idea to give them blind trust.

"As for my dogs," he went on, "you've nothing to fear. They have an even, friendly nature."

"Unless you're a scared rabbit," Mandy blurted, and for the first time, he laughed.

"Only the four-legged variety have to be concerned. Take Clancy for instance. He wasn't going to harm you. He was worrying over you. Your being up in a tree didn't strike him as an ordinary situation."

"Nor did it me." She played out a weak smile and he laughed again.

"Since you're trying to be a good sport about this, tell you what I'll do," he said. "I'll tell Grand-dad about you and maybe he'll keep the dogs away from the lodge for a while. Or give you fair warning when he's coming."

Words of thanks hovered on Mandy's lips, but the sound of the two dogs cresting the hill distracted her. She recoiled as they came bounding toward their master, skidded to a stop and wagged frenzied circles around him.

T.K. gave them a word of praise, a pat on the head, then sent them off to join Clancy in the truck. Tongues rolling to one side, they sprang to obey.

Mandy watched them cross the bridge and disappear from sight.

T.K. followed, calling back to Mandy, "Don't forget to mention me to Corey."

Mandy didn't know whether to treat that as a challenge, or if it was simply his dry brand of humor. Either way, she fully intended to follow through, first chance.

Hands skinned by the rough tree branch, she went into the lodge to wash. Catching a glimpse of her reflection in the mirror, she did a double-take. No wonder subdued amusement had danced in his eyes. She was a sight!

A small twig was caught in her tangled hair, her acorn eyes were unusually wide and her face, wearing just a hint of a tan, was smudged.

Little brown wood nut indeed! The dog had spotted her high in the limb of that red oak tree, and so had the man. So much for Dad's poetic description, she thought, pulling a face at herself in the mirror.

CHAPTER 3

FOR A DAY OR SO, Mandy watched and listened for the dogs to come prowling around the lodge, but her woodland haven remained quiet and serene. Reasoning T.K. had kept his word and explained her presence to his grandfather, Mandy settled down to sewing in earnest.

The set-up was ideal. She fell into the habit of driving out to the lodge at daybreak, working steadily until noon, taking time for a sandwich and a walk in the hills, then returning to work until evening. When her shoulders began to ache from long hours at the sewing machine, she'd pack her things away and drive back to Stratton.

Evenings were relaxed affairs, spent doing fittings, delivering finished garments or simply visiting with her family. Well aware Corey had done her a huge favor by loaning the use of the lodge, Mandy tried to be patient when, on Friday evening just as she arrived back to town, he dropped by unannounced.

"About dinner," he plunged into one of his impromptu invitations, "shall we go out for Chinese, or would you like for me to whip up one of my world famous mushroom omelets?''

Mandy kicked off her shoes and sank down on the sofa. ''Does it ever occur to you to invite me out for Friday night *before* Friday night arrives? I just got in, I haven't cleaned up yet, and for all you know, I might have other plans.''

For all her good intentions, her tone ran toward crisp. It was lost on Corey. He gave her a broad smile.

''But you don't, do you? Have other plans, I mean.''

''No. But that isn't the point.''

''I know, I know.'' His face was boyishly apologetic. ''Believe me, I don't mean to take you for granted, Mandy. It's just that I get so busy during the week, Friday's here before I know it. And my car has a will of its own. It drives me here all by itself. Honest to goodness, it does.''

A smile slipped past her effort to make a point, and with a look of relief, he stopped playing meek and humble.

''Besides, if your *other* plans involved some *other* man, I'd punch him in the nose and send him politely on his way.''

''You're impossible, do you know that?''

''Not at all,'' he argued cheerfully. ''I'm being my *most* possible, in fact. So what do you say? Chinese or glorified scrambled eggs?''

''Tacos,'' Mandy made a choice of her own. ''And give me fifteen minutes to make myself presentable.''

Eyes frank with admiration, he said, ''You're plenty presentable as it is, but if it's time you want, I'll catch the six o'clock news.''

At which point he switched on the television and made himself at home. Because it had been a warm day and she was pleasantly tired, Mandy's fifteen minutes stretched out to half an hour. She emerged from the bathroom, smelling of scented bubble-bath and dressed in a pale apricot sundress which complemented the healthy glow of her tan.

"You took your time," Corey said, "but it was worth it. You look good enough to eat."

Mandy laughed and reached for her pocketbook. "My, you *are* hungry."

His gaze lengthened. "Are you sure you've been hard at work this week? Looks to me as if you've been lazing around in the sun."

"It doesn't take much sun to turn my skin brown," Mandy said, leading the way to the door and wondering why Corey's off-handed question had half annoyed her. "Every day, just after lunch, I've been taking a walk. I adore the lodge, Corey. And the countryside surrounding it too."

"Good. I'm glad it's working out for you."

"Oh!" Mandy stopped so suddenly, Corey just escaped stepping on her heels. "I almost forgot. I told Claire Manson I'd drop off her caftan if I finished it today. And I did."

"Can't it wait until tomorrow?" Corey tried to nudge her out the door, but she stood her ground.

"No, I promised. It won't take five minutes, Corey."

"Is that a promise too?"

"Count on it. I'll buy dinner if it takes a single second longer."

That riled him, as she knew it would, for if Corey was rigid in any respect, it was with regard to a man's role in the dating game. Any whisper of dutch treat put him on his high horse.

Mandy sat next to the passenger's door, smiling to herself as he ran on about how he'd sooner starve than let a girl buy *his* dinner.

Claire's Cadillac was parked on the paved horseshoe drive in front of her modern tri-level house in Stratton's swankiest subdivision.

"Are you coming in?" Mandy asked as she got out of the car.

"No. I'll wait here. Five minutes, remember?"

"Keep the meter running," she teased, then started up to Claire's door, the plastic garment bag containing Claire's caftan folded over her arm.

Claire was quick to answer the bell, then spent a moment raving over Mandy's skill before writing her a check.

"Is that Corey with you?" she asked, as Mandy thanked her and turned away.

"Yes, it is," Mandy said, mildly surprised that Claire's full red mouth was shaped in a petulant frown.

"You won't mind if I say hello?"

"Of course not," Mandy murmured, then started back to the car with Claire at her side, her silver sandals slapping purposefully against her heels.

It was with seeming reluctance that Corey rolled down his window to return Claire's greeting.

"I thought you had a business trip this weekend," Claire purred past an artificial smile.

"Cancelled at the last minute," was Corey's smooth reply. He tossed Mandy a warning glance. She smiled sweetly.

Far be it from her to inform Claire he seldom went out of town. Knowing Claire to be a chase and a flirt, she almost felt sorry for Corey as he tried, verbally at least, to shake her off his window.

"I wish we had time," he declined Claire's offer of a cold drink, "but Mandy and I have reservations for six-forty-five."

Claire contradicted her cloudy expression with a sunny, "Have a nice evening, then. And, Corey?" She paused. Her gaze cut to Mandy then back to Corey. "Don't be such a stranger. You make a great mushroom omelet."

As soon as the car was rolling again, Mandy

recovered enough to say with mild reproach, "Reservations? At Taco Johns?"

Corey said, as if he expected some major explosion, "Now before you bring in the hanging jury, let me explain."

"About the mushroom omelet? There's no need. You're a free agent. And besides, she's right. You *do* make a great mushroom omelet."

"You aren't angry?" His eyes left the road long enough to give her face an anxious search.

"No, of course not," Mandy said. And it was true. She wasn't the least angry or jealous or even too terribly surprised. It explained why she hadn't heard a word from Corey all week. Hadn't she often told herself Corey enjoyed women far too much to limit himself to just one?

"It's good of you to take it so well," Corey muttered, his expression morose. Overall, he appeared depressed rather than relieved by her reaction.

"Smile, Corey." Mandy reached across the seat and patted his hand. "You'll get frown wrinkles. Besides, it's a lovely evening and I intend to enjoy myself."

And enjoy she did, feasting on crumbly hard-shelled tacos, drinking down a tall icy Coke and hearing all about Corey's busy week. To her amusement, he carefully avoided any mention of Claire.

Feeling content and introspective, Mandy was quiet all the way home. It wasn't until she and Corey were saying good-night that she remembered to ask about T.K. Cooke.

"By the way," she said, fitting her key to the lock on her apartment door, "I met a friend of yours this week."

"Oh? Who might that be?"

She swung the door open. "T.K. Cooke."

"Tommy? You're kidding!"

Mandy switched on the light, and was startled to

find Corey looking more than a little upset. The reason eluded her, for her mind was wrestling with some unknown factor here that, like the clue to a puzzle, wouldn't fall into place.

"He introduced himself as T.K. I suppose the T stands for Thomas. Anyway," she rushed on. "It was quite a coincidence because it wasn't actually the first time we'd met. Last Friday he came to my rescue in Danny's market. There was a German shepherd parked at the door, and you know how timid I am about dogs. Well, your friend was kind enough to escort me past the dog. In fact, he gave me a lift home. Keep in mind now, that's rescue number one."

Dropping her pocketbook on the sofa, Mandy launched into her second meeting with T.K. Cooke, peppering the telling with humor, despite that, at the time, it had seemed nothing short of catastrophic.

"At any rate," she wound to a close, little aware of Corey's grim-set mouth, "T.K. must by this time be certain I'm a hopeless case where dogs are concerned."

Corey was still at the door, frowning darkly. Over what, she couldn't imagine.

"What is it, Corey? Aren't you and this T.K. fellow on friendly terms?"

"Mandy, don't you know who T.K. Cooke is?"

"No. Should I?"

"He's my partner."

Her lips shaped a small, soundless, "Oh!" as the significance of Corey's words hit home. She went stock still, recalling how haughtily she'd informed the man he was on private property. All at once, it was as if everything—even the tacos!—had turned on her. Feeling sick, she slumped back against the sofa cushions.

"But he can't be!"

"I'm afraid he is."

"He didn't *say* he was your partner. And the way I

46

took him to task for letting his dogs run on private property, he should by all rights have thrown his identity into my face. Corey, I was at my most high handed, most ghastly worst!''

A weak grin failed to do any more than touch Corey's lips before dying. ''That's just like him, not telling you. I'd imagine he's enjoying the last laugh. You needn't look so devastated, though. He didn't run you off for trespassing, did he?''

''I wasn't trespassing!'' she said, indignation sparking amber lights in her eyes. ''You gave me your permission. You told him I was going to use the lodge a couple of weeks.'' She paused, not liking his evasive expression. ''Didn't you?''

''I tried, but I couldn't reach him.'' Corey sat down beside her and tried to take her hand. Full of recriminations, she leapt to her feet and paced around the small living room.

''How could I have behaved so badly? It would be bad enough if he'd been expecting me, but there I was the trespasser accusing him of trespassing on his own property!''

''Calm down, Mandy. It isn't the end of the world.''

She snapped out of her own preoccupation long enough to note Corey was looking awfully glum despite his attempts to reassure her.

''When did you say he was returning from his trip?''

Scowling, Corey replied, ''I don't recall telling you he was *on* a trip.''

Mandy caught her lip between small white teeth. ''I guess it was he who told me. Let's see—he said three or four weeks. That means he couldn't possibly return any sooner than two weeks. I can promise you, I'll be gone from the lodge before he returns!''

''If that's the way you want it,'' Corey gave her no cause for argument. He came to her then and lay a hand on her shoulder, turning her to face him.

47

"Mandy, I'm sorry about the mix-up. To tell you the truth, I'm a lot sorrier than you realize. Tommy's the kind of guy women lose their hearts to and he seldom even notices they exist. I haven't been all that anxious for you to meet him."

"Why?" she asked, though she didn't need to really—the answer was in the possessive way his eyes roamed her features.

He touched the shallow dimple in her chin. "Let's just say I didn't want to see you get hurt."

"You needn't have worried." Mandy stepped away from him. "I wouldn't think of trying to compete with those dogs of his."

"Still, I'm sorry this happened. I expected you'd be in and out of the lodge with Tommy none the wiser."

She turned narrowed eyes on him. "You didn't even try to contact him, did you Corey? You just let me set up shop there, thinking what he didn't know wouldn't hurt him!"

"No, that isn't so. I *did* try to call Tommy. Several times Sunday evening and then very early Monday morning. But I couldn't reach him. He must have been out with the dogs."

"Yeah," Mandy said dryly. "Talking me down out of a tree. Corey, I hate this kind of situation! Maybe I'll get my things from the lodge tomorrow and not go back."

"There's no need for you to do that. Really Mandy. You're taking this too much to heart. I should have planned things better, but with Tommy's flight to Chicago scheduled for Monday, I didn't think there was any way the two of you would meet."

"I still feel dreadful."

"There isn't any reason to. Tommy takes things in stride."

"Tommy?" Mandy rolled the name off, testing it and finding it ill-suited for the man. "Why do you keep calling him Tommy?"

For the first time since they'd entered her apartment, Corey flashed a genuine grin. "Mostly because it irritates him, and he's not all that easy to irritate."

"Why would you want to?"

"Because he has that unshakable quality about him, and it challenges me to try to unsettle him."

Puzzled by his brooding look, Mandy gave her head a shake. "I don't understand you, Corey. I'd think if there was anyone in this world you really needed to get along with, it'd be your partner."

"That's because you don't know Tommy." Eyes brooding, he added, "He's one of those guys who has had a golden slice of life passed his way. Know what I mean?"

When Mandy let silence serve as an answer, Corey elaborated.

"His father was a corporation lawyer, good at what he did, and raking in plenty of money. That alone was enough to assure Tommy of a posh set up."

"But that wasn't all?" Mandy felt more curiosity over Corey's reaction to T.K. Cooke than actual interest in the man's personal life.

"No. His mother." He paused, debated his choice of words and finished with a tense, "Let's just say she was born rich, lived rich and died rich."

"Died?"

"That's right. Tommy's parents were killed in a boating accident several years back. Guess who inherited?"

"T.K., I would imagine."

"That's right. Good old Tommy. Rough life, huh?"

"Are you jealous, Corey?" Mandy's thoughts leaked into words.

"No, not really. But just once, it might be interesting to see him leveled like the rest of us who came up the hard way." He turned then and left without another word.

It was a side to Corey she didn't much like. And

49

later, much later as time is measured by sleepless tossing, she was still wondering about him. He usually seemed so congenial, so happy-go-lucky so . . . invigorating.

This volatile twist she'd viewed made her uneasy. Was it simply that T.K. was a "have" and Corey was a "have not" that brought out the explosive quality? No. That wasn't even true. For a young man, Corey had accomplished a great deal in his life, both personal and business.

Wasn't he an equal partner in Four Seasons Pet Supply Manufacturing? In her book, that was quite an accomplishment, especially since the other half of the partnership had inherited his buying power.

She tossed her leg out over the sheet and tried to get comfortable. All things said and done, Corey and T.K. must have a very strange business relationship. Very strange indeed.

On Sunday afternoon, Mandy took her father out to the country and showed off her private hideaway. Perhaps it was because her mother had died when she was young that such a strong bond existed between father and daughter. It mattered not if they talked in bubbling flows, their words spilling over one another, or if they shared a quiet mood. The feeling of companionship was ever secure.

Passing through a scrubby stand of oaks and hickory, Mandy thought how her father moved with the drive and energy of a much younger man. He loved the country too, and she was glad to spend her afternoon just roaming the woods with him.

Sensitive to the change in terrain, Mandy paused to catch her breath. "This is farther than I've ever come from the lodge. Mercy, it's getting hot, isn't it?"

Robert Holt wiped his brow and returned his handkerchief to the pocket of his slacks. "Our cool spring days are behind us, I fear. Look, a prickly pear cactus. I'd say we're coming to a glade."

He loped ahead and over the hill. Enduring the catch in her side, Mandy pushed on close behind and soon saw he was right. A miniature prairie nestled in rock-bound hills spread before them.

Because of the thin rocky soil, the wide varieties of oaks common to the Ozarks gave way entirely to prairie grasses and an occasional shallow-rooted juniper. The early spring flowers had already bloomed. But the prairie rose smiled in rocky cracks and crevices as did the prickly pear cactus.

Her father stood drinking in the view. "It's like a piece of western prairie blown right onto our doorstep, isn't it?

Mandy smiled and jogged his memory. "I've never seen the western prairies, Dad, but I'll take your word for it."

"Your mother and I took our honeymoon in South Dakota. Did I ever tell you?"

He had, but Mandy didn't stop him from telling her again. She loved to hear him speak of the days when her mother had been strong and healthy and their marriage new. He spoke of her as if she'd just stepped out of the room for a second, and it revived Mandy's own memory until she too could remember the shine in her mother's blue eyes and the soft southern sound of her voice.

Dropping down on a boulder at the edge of the glade, Mandy murmured, "You never get over missing a loved one, do you Dad."

"No. No, you don't." His eyes scanned the glade. "But death lost its terror for me a long time ago. Look around you, Mandy. How everything is alive and green and growing. Soon summer drought will come. The sun will scorch the grasses and burn the rocky soil until everything is brown and dead looking. It would seem no amount of rain could green it up again.

"But next spring, the flowers will come. The grass will flourish. And each year we appreciate it all the more for the starkness of the dry season.

"Death is like that too. At first it hurts so badly, we feel we'll crumble beneath the pain, that no good can come of it."

Mandy looked into his serene face, thinking how strange it was to be speaking of death with so much life around them. She sifted a straggling clump of grass through her fingers as her father resumed talking.

"But God promised a resurrection to those who have confessed His son as Savior, and to those who haven't, as well. Because of that promise, those in Christ look forward to a great reunion. The tears that fall over the loss of a loved one are like rain. They green up our lives again."

"Still, it's hard not to wonder why God took her when she was so young." Mandy thought of the first months after her mother's death. "Does it ever make you . . ." she searched for a gentler word and found none, ". . . angry?"

"It's natural to wonder and to be hurt, even angry over the loss. But you know, once I stopped asking why and began thanking God for the good years, for the memories I still cherish and for the two lives born of our unity, it was easier. The anger died and I could remember without that crushing feeling of loss."

It was a familiar statement of her father's—how God could bring good things out of bad. Mulling it over in her mind, Mandy got lost in her own private thoughts until her father said with marked reluctance, "We'd better start back. I have a stack of final exams to grade before tomorrow."

Mandy wrinkled her nose, and he laughed. "No more pleasant for the teacher than the student, I assure you."

She considered arguing the point, then stopped short when the breeze carried the sound of barking dogs. Latching on to her father's arm she said, "It's those same dogs, I'll bet. Remember, the ones I told you about?'' she added, for over Sunday dinner she'd told her father and Gram and Ellen all about T.K. Cooke and his dogs as well as his connection to Corey.

Her father chuckled as he lay a hand over hers. ''Relax, Mandy. I have a way with dogs.''

''It isn't just the dogs,'' she confided as the sound of barking drew nearer. ''It's him. Land, I hope it *isn't* him! He isn't supposed to return for two or three weeks.''

''It could be anyone. Beagles on a scent sound pretty much alike,'' her father pointed out, maintaining his attitude of calm.

Three dogs barreled past and disappeared in the direction of the glade. Mandy relaxed her hold on her father's arm.

He smiled gently. ''Dogs are supposed to be man's best friend, remember?

Mandy shuddered. ''I'll have to be pretty hard up for a friend before I cozy up to a dog.''

Worry wrinkles furrowed his brow. ''It's been a long time, Mandy. Can't you put it behind you?''

Though he didn't add, ''This fear of yours isn't natural,'' his expression mirrored the thought as visibly as the scars on her leg bore witness to the founding of her phobia those long years ago.

Twenty-one stitches it had taken to close up the wounds put there by a dog. Not just any dog. A dog she'd trusted. What could she say? That she'd try? Hadn't she tried before and given up, thinking it was something she'd just have to live with. After all, other folks had phobias. Fear of heights. Fear of small places. Fear of snakes and rats and spiders, even. She wasn't such an odd-ball. And, as long as the fear didn't interfere with her life, what difference did it make?

''You know,'' her father brought her out of her thoughts, ''when I was a boy I had a beagle myself. Paintbrush. Now how's that for an original name?''

"These poets—they start out young."

He laughed, as he always did when she called him a poet. "He did look like he'd had an unfortunate encounter with a paint brush. None of the normal beagle markings. I guess if you want to name names, he was a mutt. But he sure could hunt."

"*You* hunted? You've never mentioned it before."

He said, "Most boys who grow up in the hills do hunt. It's a way of life."

"I think it's barbaric. Sort of, anyway." She softened her view, lest she hurt his feelings.

"You sound like your mother," he said. "She had an aversion to hunting too. Though I noticed she was able to wring the neck of a stewing chicken without batting an eye."

"That's different," Mandy was quick to insert.

"Is it?" A small smile played at the corners of his mouth. "After we were first married, I brought home a rabbit to cook. Your mother cooked it all right. She even made a stab at eating it. But halfway through dinner, I saw she had tears in her eyes. She said she felt like she was eating Peter Rabbit."

"I can understand that," Mandy said, though she was hard pressed not to laugh, thinking her mother had sure pulled one over on him.

"Can you now?" His voice climbed defensively. "Then tell me, did you ever feel, as Gram serves Sunday dinner, like you're eating Chicken Little. Or the Little Red Hen, perhaps."

"Chickens are just chickens."

"Face it, Mandy. God made the animals for man, not the other way around. As long as we're good stewards . . ."

"Okay, okay." Starting to grin, Mandy held up a hand in truce. "If that is your view, you're welcome to it."

He was looking so pleased with himself, she couldn't resist adding, "You Mr. MacGregor, you."

Her father's laughter faded as they caught sight of a wiry old man puffing and panting his way up the hill toward them. At his heels trotted yet another beagle.

Mandy reclaimed her father's arm. The timid gesture must have given her away, for the white-haired gentleman stopped short and ordered the dog to sit.

Without prelude, he then thrust forth a gnarled, work-worn hand. "You must be Amanda Holt."

Nodding, she accepted his handshake.

"T.K. told me to keep an eye out for you," he said. "I'm Kyle, and mighty pleased to meet you, though if I'd known you'd be out and about today, I'd of walked the dogs elsewhere."

Assuming him to be the grandfather T.K. had made reference to, Mandy was quick to say, "But that isn't necessary. *I'm* the one who's intruding. You mustn't inconvenience yourself because of me."

His faded blue eyes twinkled. "Inconvenience, you say? When there's plenty of hills to roam? No Missy, it's no inconvenience at all."

"That's very kind of you, Mr. Kyle."

He laughed a throaty laugh. "Not so formal, Missy. It's Kyle, just plain Kyle."

"You are T.K.'s grandfather, aren't you?" Mandy made certain. "He mentioned you when we met the other day. This is my father, Robert Holt."

"Pleased to meet you."

While the men shook hands, Mandy tossed the dog a nervous glance. He was fidgeting, his ears like soft brown shoe-tongues lifting and dropping at the sound of their voices. Mandy backed off a step or two.

Alert to her movement, the old man used a kind voice. "You're safe, Missy. This here's Clancy. Friendliest rascal ever to sport brown eyes and a tail."

"We've met." Mandy cast the dog a mistrustful glance. His tail thumped the ground.

Her father said, "It'll take a lot more than a tail wagging to win this girl over, fella. When she was little a stray we'd taken in got the best of her. She's been holding a grudge since."

As her father petted the dog, Mandy drew in her bottom lip. His explanation sounded so simple, when in reality, the turmoil dogs wrought in her was very complex.

The old man kept a considering gaze upon her. "It happens that way sometimes. When I was a lad, a fella I knew got kicked by a mule. He up and sold that mule right off and even though he had to plow his field by hand, I don't think he was ever sorry he'd done it."

He gave her a warm wink and a smile that seemed to say he'd accept her the way she was. Right then and there, she decided he'd make a good friend for life.

Perhaps that was why it seemed quite natural for him to say as they parted ways, "Maybe I'll stop by the lodge and pay you a visit some day soon. Clancy's fair company, but I still get kind of lonesome with the boy gone."

"Why don't you come tomorrow? Around lunch time," Mandy invited. "Can I count on you to eat a couple of sandwiches and finish off a box of girlscout cookies that are in danger of going stale?"

"You bet. Kyle Cooke isn't one to turn down a lunch date with a lady pretty as you."

He winked again and tipped his cap, then called to Clancy who'd wandered off to investigate a butterfly.

"What a nice old man," Mandy said, as they walked on.

"Yes, he seems to be. But I thought your purpose in coming way out here to work was to get away from distractions and interruptions."

Mistrusting the sly look he slanted her way, Mandy said, "I don't think Mr. Cooke will make a nuisance of himself."

Her father's grin made her increasingly uneasy. "Just going to wait around for T.K. Cooke to return?" he suggested.

"I suppose I owe the man an apology. Yes, I'll stay long enough to pay it. Then, I'm gone."

"Like Goldilocks caught red handed in the cottage of the Three Bears?"

Needled in spite of herself, Mandy lifted her chin. "I could be wrong about you. Maybe poetry isn't your calling at all. You certainly seem to have a preoccupation with fairy tales."

She gave her head a toss and ran ahead, her father's laughter chasing after her.

CHAPTER 4

Spring was giving way to summer and though the lodge was well shaded, Mandy opened all the windows as well as the door, trying to coax in a cooling breeze.

The morning passed swiftly. She was still at her sewing machine, surrounded by yards and yards of ivory taffeta when Kyle Cooke showed up at noon.

"Anyone home?" he hollered.

Mandy shot her chair back and turned toward the door. "Come on in!"

To her dismay, Clancy was with the old man. He trotted right toward Ellen's wedding dress.

"Out, Clancy," the old man ordered. "You weren't invited."

Mandy's heart steadied as the dog slunk out the door step and dropped down on the concrete. His gaze followed the old man in, and Kyle flashed a sheepish grin.

"I tried to sneak away, but he just doesn't get outfoxed often. The silly critter has stuck so close lately, it's a wonder I haven't tripped and tangled myself around him. Reckon he thinks I'm a helpless codger in need of his watch-care?"

The dog was obviously protective of the old man, and for Kyle's sake, Mandy was glad. Should he ever be in need of help, the dog looked capable of rousing it.

"Just let me clear one end of this table and we'll have lunch," Mandy said, and proceeded to carefully drape the bridal gown makings over several chairs.

Lunch consisted of sandwiches, fresh fruit, girl scout cookies and sun tea. If it had been a gourmet meal, Kyle couldn't have eaten with any more relish.

Conversation was cordial. Mandy found herself admitting, "When I found that Corey had neglected to tell your grandson about my using the lodge, I thought perhaps I ought to move my things out right away. I mean, I hate to be thought of as the pushy type who . . ."

"No, no!" Kyle interrupted. "T.K. doesn't mind your being here. The lodge is sitting empty and unused. Anyway, any friend of Corey's is a friend of his."

Detecting a note of cynicism, Mandy lifted her head, and proceeded with care. "Corey's told me so little about T.K. I guess it seems odd to say I've known Corey for over a year, yet didn't realize when I met T.K. last week that he was Corey's partner. Corey's always referred to his partner as "Tommy," so I suppose that is the reason I didn't make the connection automatically."

"Tommy." Kyle spat the name in distaste. "That sounds like Corey. I don't suppose he bothered to mention he and T.K. are . . ."

Kyle stopped short, his honest open features closing up like a window slamming shut. He walked over to give a scrap of sandwich to Clancy at the door.

"Are what?" Mandy prompted, curious beyond reason.

"Partners," Kyle finished. "I don't suppose he told you that because he likes to play the big shot. You know, get all the notoriety for Four Seasons Pet Supply Manufacturing. As if the idea and money behind it are his."

"He's never said that," Mandy murmured out of loyalty to Corey. "He's never said much at all about how the company got started. Just that he and Tommy, I mean T.K., got together on it when they finished their stint in the army."

Kyle turned from the dog to look at her and something in his expression made her ask, "Isn't that right?"

"Roughly."

That was all he said on the subject. It wasn't long before he said he would be moving along. Mandy invited him to come again soon and he assured her he would.

She watched him cross the bridge with the dog and her curiosity lingered. Kyle Cooke did not like Corey and that surprised her. Corey usually drew people to him with his smooth charm and his gusto for life.

Perhaps it was some trite thing that had turned the old man against Corey. Lacking the time or the patience to think it through, Mandy went back to her sewing.

After his first visit, Kyle fell into the habit of dropping by daily. Over the next two weeks, Mandy never knew when to expect him. As T.K. had said, he wasn't a man to be ruled by a clock. One thing never changed. The dog was always with him, though after the first time, he never again had to be told to come no further than the door step.

Mandy got accustomed to seeing him there. Perhaps his presence was therapy of a sort. His loyal guarding of the old man touched her.

That Kyle came from the old school where pride in workmanship was of great importance was evidenced by his consideration for her work. It seemed to impress him that she'd designed Ellen's wedding dress herself and he watched with interest as she put it together.

"Don't let me bother you," he'd say time and again as he looked on from a nearby chair. "Keep right on working."

When he tired of watching, he'd take a block of wood and a pocket-knife and start whittling. However, when he'd rise to go, he'd have nothing to show for his work but a pile of shavings.

"Botched it again," he'd say with a faded wink, and she soon caught on he had no yearning to create. He simply liked the busy feel of a knife in his hand and the sight of wood shavings drifting to the floor.

Generally, he was so quiet, she nearly forgot he was on the place. When he did talk, it was of the dogs, his vegetable patch, or his grandson.

The dog talk flowed over her, though she wouldn't have hurt his feelings by openly showing her distaste for the topic. They often compared notes on gardening, Gram's garden versus his. And when he spoke of T.K., an odd feeling always came over her. It was as if she was coming to know the man through his grandfather.

Kyle spoke openly of T.K.'s father. When his daughter-in-law was mentioned, he usually clammed up. All Mandy learned was that the woman, rich in her own right, had founded a line of cosmetics that did extremely well. So Corey was right on one score—wealth had come easily to T.K. Cooke.

On Thursday, the fifth of June, Mandy sewed the pearl beading to the lace bodice of Ellen's taffeta gown. Thrilled with the finished result, she called it a day early and drove back to town for Ellen's final fitting.

Ellen turned excited pirouettes, watching her reflection in the mirror and almost making Mandy dizzy just looking on!

"You're going to have to stand still if you expect me to get the hem pinned straight," she warned for the third time.

"I can't stand still! Mandy, it's gorgeous. You've done such a super job. Just look! Aren't you just bursting with pride!"

Admittedly, she was modestly pleased with the result of her labors. The cathedral-length gown, the taffeta flounce at the hemline and the leg of mutton sleeves were perfect for Ellen's tall, willowy figure. And the pearl beading on lace was a fragile, finishing touch. She grinned and admitted, "You're gorgeous, Ellen. And you know it, too. Poor Gregory. You'll give him an awful time."

"No, I won't. I love him too much to be anything *but* beautiful. Pretty is as pretty does, as Gram would say." She did another twirl and caught Mandy in a hug.

The last couple of days, it seemed to Mandy that Ellen's excitement had reached a feverish pitch. She was privately a bit worried. Could anyone maintain such high spirits for an indefinite amount of time without crashing back to reality?

"There's a lot more to a marriage than a lovely wedding," she warned mildly.

Ellen wrinkled her nose and laughed. "How would you know? Come on, be happy with me. Don't fuss."

"I *am* happy. With you, for you, the whole works. But you'd better settle down. Gregory's going to have to chain you to earth or you're going to float right on up to the clouds."

Ellen just laughed, and Mandy gave up trying to calm her, pinned the hem as carefully as she could, and for once, was glad to see Ellen go. Whew! Just being in the same room with her took her breath away. When she fell in love (if?) she hoped she'd exercise a little better rein on her emotions.

The next day, knowing it to be her last at the lodge,

Mandy packed a picnic hamper and determined to fetch Kyle if he didn't show up by noon. The picnic would be a farewell gesture. How she'd miss the old man!

To her disappointment, the sky was overcast. But after all the beautiful weather they'd had, how could she complain? It made her think of a verse Gram was fond of quoting—"This is the day the Lord has made. Let us rejoice and be glad in it."

Painstakingly hemming the voluminous skirt of Ellen's bridal gown, Mandy began to hum a song which put the words of Gram's verse to music. Before long, the words spilled out until the empty lodge threw back in echoes the clear, sweet sound of her voice.

Now and again, the sun would peek through the clouds and glimmer in patches upon the floor. Nimble fingers stitching, head bowed, Mandy fluctuated between snatches of old familiar songs. She was into a rousing camp song when the sound of Clancy's familiar bark brought her up short. Knotting her final thread, she reached for the scissors and spoke without turning.

"It doesn't sound as if Clancy thinks much of my singing." she laughed and went on. "I'm so glad you came. I packed this monster of a picnic. Sort of a farewell to paradise. This is my last day at the lodge."

A shadow was thrown over her work, the length of it a warning even before she lifted her head to find, not the kindly old man she'd expected, but T.K. Cooke.

Upturned face quick to color, Mandy's heart skipped a beat as she met his smoky grey expression. "I thought you were Kyle."

"That warm welcome wasn't meant for me? Somehow I thought not."

He was taller than she remembered, his body lean and muscular. And his mouth was being held straight

63

by an effort. Mandy shifted in her chair. "Kyle drops by most days, so naturally when I heard Clancy bark, I thought it was him."

"He's been beating my time, has he?"

The words, once out, seemed to surprise him almost as much as they did Mandy. Or had they? she wondered, detecting an imp of mischief dancing in his eyes.

She averted her face. What was it about this man that made her feel so gauche? And how did he always manage to catch her in the midst of something awkward?

He must have guessed at her discomfort, for the lines of amusement deepened. "Don't feel too badly. I surprised Grand-dad too. There must have been half a dozen dogs in the house, and I'm a firm believer dogs belong outdoors."

He made a little chuckling noise, trying to coax a smile, yet Mandy sat as silent as the machine in front of her. She cut the final thread off Ellen's wedding gown and fit it over a padded hanger.

Though her back was to him, she sensed the strength of his scrutiny. What was he thinking? That she was one nervy lady, moving in, setting up shop, not caring the least she had the permission of only half a partnership?

How foolish she'd been! She shouldn't be here, had no *right* to be here at all! Why hadn't he been straightforward with her? Why hadn't he made his identity clear the day he'd rescued her from the branches of that red oak tree?

"A wedding dress?" He broke into her mental agony with a question.

She nodded without turning and secured a garment bag over the dress to keep out dust particles.

"It's lovely," he said quietly. "Did you by chance design it yourself?"

Again she let a nod suffice.

"You must be very talented," he said.

His comments distracted her. With difficulty she turned the conversation around. "I've been trying to frame an apology every since Corey told me you were his partner. I was rude that day in the woods and it was unforgivable of me." She hesitated, then gave in to her curiosity. "Why didn't you tell me you owned the land too? That you were Corey's partner?"

"I didn't think it was important at the time."

"And your name," she plowed on. "What is it, really? T.K? Thomas? Tommy?"

"Thomas Kyle, after my father and grandfather. Confusing, you see. Thus, the abbreviating initials." Explanation finished, he kept his steady gaze on her and asked a question of his own.

"It isn't Corey, is it?"

Baffled, Mandy said, "What isn't Corey?"

He gestured toward the dress. "What I meant to ask is are you engaged to Corey?"

"Engaged?" Sweeping a loose curl back from her face, Mandy gazed back at him in puzzlement. "Oh! You mean the dress! No. No, it isn't Corey."

Before she could add that it wasn't even her dress, he said, "I didn't see how it could be Corey. I mean, he's pretty free about throwing his lady friends' names around and to my knowledge, he's never mentioned you. Then it occurred to me that could be significant."

It gave her a wry sense of pleasure having *him* misunderstand for a change. Smoothing the wrinkles in the garment bag, Mandy drew the moment out.

"I should think, when Corey marries, it will be the event of the season. He likes to do things with a big splash."

"So you and Corey are just friends?" he questioned.

"Yes. Good friends." She picked up scattered straight pins and dropped them in her pin box.

"You never did say why you were using the lodge."

Hiding a small smile, she tucked her scissors into her sewing box. "No, I guess I didn't, did I?"

His eyes narrowed. "When's the wedding?"

"Later this month."

Voice edged with an inexplicable emotion, he scanned the length of the lodge with all-seeing grey eyes. "You're here alone?"

Disliking the subtle insinuation in his voice, Mandy said a bit tartly, "Yes, I'm alone."

He turned innocent eyes on her again. "I didn't know. These days, some folks get the honeymoon and the wedding out of order, so to speak."

Crimson flagging her cheeks, she came to full stature. "That may be *some* folks' way, but I assure you, it isn't mine."

Grinning at the reaction he'd stirred, T.K. raised his hands as if to fend off a punch. "Take it easy. I'm just making polite conversation."

"Polite?"

"It started off polite." He gave a little ground, having the good grace to look contrite. "But when you side-stepped all my questions, I tried a new approach. You still haven't given me a straight answer."

The fun had gone out of the exchange and the joke, albeit a bad one, had turned on her. Mandy said, "The wedding is June twenty-seventh. It's my sister's, not mine. As for Corey letting me use the lodge, it was so I could get away from interruptions and catch up on my sewing. Any more questions I failed to answer?"

"Just one." His face relaxed and he appeared suddenly cheerful. "Would you consider sharing that picnic lunch with me, since Grand-dad can't make it? Let's say we're celebrating your broken engagement."

"There never was an . . ." Mandy stopped short,

realizing she was being teased. "I don't know," she said in truth. "We seem to hit off sparks."

"Where would the world be without sparks?"

It wasn't a question that required an answer, yet it made her all the more keenly aware of the emotional tension she felt toward him. It was an element lacking in her relationship with Corey, this spark that could kindle a flame, perhaps rage out of control. But no, she was smarter than that.

"So what do you say?" he coaxed. "Are you going to share your lunch?"

"What fun is a picnic alone?" she capitulated with the beginnings of a smile.

Grinning back, he took the wicker basket from the table and started toward the door. "I know a good spot, if you're willing to take a chance on getting caught in the rain."

"It does look like it could pour," she agreed, side-stepping Clancy to get out the door. "How about under the red oak there?"

"No, not there. That tree isn't safe." Laughing at her wide-eyed look, he closed Clancy into the lodge. "I was standing under that tree not long ago and it dropped a girl instead of acorns."

Blushing and trying not to appear taken in by his teasing, Mandy said, "Let's live dangerously. Where's this good spot of yours?"

"Just follow me, your trusty scout." He gave her a mock salute, then caught her hand in his as if he had a perfect right.

Leading the way over a hill and through a cool shady forest of oaks and pines, maples and beach trees, he said, "In the Ozarks, you're constantly reminded the earth is made of rocks. Even on the forest floor, they come cropping through."

She nodded in agreement. The beauty of a winding stream blocked by rocks and slowed to a trickle caught at her heart, making her want to skip and run like a child. Hampered as she was by a full gathered pink skirt and flat sandals, it was all she could do to keep stride with T.K.

"You mentioned this being your last day," T.K. said, as they walked on, watching the flight of birds overhead. "Any particular reason?"

"When Corey lent me the use of the lodge, he asked that I be out before this weekend. Something about your having plans for the use of it this weekend."

"Me?" He shot her a quizzical glance.

"That's what he said. Why? Don't you?"

"I don't know what gave him that idea. I wasn't even sure I'd be back."

He stopped then as they came to a small clearing. Some twenty-odd feet up a bluff, ferns cascaded over an outcropping of rock. Mandy thought it a beautiful spot for a picnic and said so. Seeming pleased, T.K. helped her spread a checkered cloth and unload the picnic basket.

Watching her unwrap the sandwiches, he said, "If the lodge is working out for you and you'd like to stay longer, you're welcome."

"I don't know," she murmured. "I'll have to think it over." And between bites of ham sandwiches, nibbles of chips, and long drinks of cold lemonade, she considered and reconsidered his offer.

Just as they were finishing lunch, the first rain-drops fell. T.K. turned his face skyward and remarked, "I think they mean business."

Hurriedly reloading the hamper, Mandy cried, "We're going to get drenched!"

He laughed and caught her arm. "Up the trail, there's a cave. See the opening behind the ferns?"

The ferns made such thick curtains, Mandy had to take his word for it. Her mood of exhilaration triggered by his, she laughed too.

"All right, lead the way. But I'm warning you, these sandals weren't made for climbing. If I fall, I'm taking you down with me."

His hand was warm and moist in hers as he pulled her along the steep path. Raindrops pattered down, glistening on his dark hair like tiny prisms. He climbed with the sure-footed ease of a mountain goat. Mandy found it hard to follow. Halfway up, she stumbled. The rocks were slippery from the rain and her flat-soled sandals impossible foot-gear.

"Go on," she urged. "There's no need in both of us getting drenched. I'll find an easier way up."

He darted up a big rock, set the basket down and squatted to reach for her hands. "Come on. I'll lift you up."

Mandy shook her head, but he latched on to her wrists and wouldn't let go. The chilly rain acting as a tonic spurred a wrecklessness in her. Laughing she tossed her shoes up to him.

The rocks were tough beneath her tender feet, but she found foot-holds and with T.K.'s strong-armed assistance, made it to the cave opening, thoroughly damp but in good spirits.

Their laughter mixed together as they dashed in out of the rain. The antechamber of the cave was fifteen feet tall, perhaps taller. Mandy squinted in the semi-darkness. The smoke of many campfires had darkened the ceiling. Overhead, there was a crack like a natural chimney, letting in a ribbon of light.

While he found a dry spot for the hamper, Mandy slipped into her sandals and asked, "How far back does it go?"

"Five miles, anyway."

"You've explored it?"

"Only the more accessible parts. Grand-dad brought me here one summer when I'd come to visit. I must have been about twelve, just ripe for adventure."

"You explored it *alone?*"

Amused by her tone of disapproval, he chuckled. "No, Grand-dad went with me. I might have been better off alone. He was real good at giving me the shivers, telling tales of runaway slaves hiding out here, of Indian hunting parties sheltering, waiting for the weather to lift, of outlaws running from the long arm of the law.''

"Were the stories true?'' Mandy asked, her voice dropping to a whisper.

A half-smile visible in the dim light, he took her hand again and gave it a squeeze. "True, everyone of them, I'm sure. Are you scared?''

Hearing the laughter in his voice, she drew away with a stout, "Don't be silly. Even if they're true stories, that was a long time ago.''

"Yes. But keep in mind, when you get back in the cave on a breezy day, you can hear whining voices.''

"The wind finding its way through cracks and crevices, I'd imagine.'' Still, an involuntary out-break of goose-flesh crept up her arms.

"Sensible you are, like Grand-dad. A lot of fun *you'd* be in a cave!'' He laughed as he went to the cave opening to peer out through trailing ferns.

"Still raining,'' he said, coming back to her. He took the checkered cloth from the wicker basket. "We might as well wait it out in comfort.''

Mandy helped him spread it on a dry piece of cave floor, where the wall offered a back-rest of sorts. Then she sat beside him, listening until he'd exhausted his cave stories.

"What's the cave like? Deep inside, I mean?'' she asked.

His voice was low and smooth, easy to listen to, making her see the cave as he spoke of clay floors that stuck to shoes like glue, then turned treacherous on steep grades; of pools of water deep within the cave where blind colorless cave fish swam; of the darkness that was totally empty of light, blacker than the blackest night.

Perhaps it was the peppering rain outside and the

silence within that gave them a feeling of being cut-off from the world and drew them close enough to share confidences. Until the rain ended, he told her of his childhood.

"I grew up in Kansas City," he said, stretching out on the checkered cloth, bending his elbow to prop his head in his hand, and watching her shadowy face as he talked. "My father's law firm was there, as well as Mother's cosmetic business. We didn't get away from the city often. My mother had a child from a previous marriage and since she had weekend visiting rights, she never wanted to leave on the weekend. Dad was tied down with his job, so the result was I saw very little of Grand-dad when I was real young.

"But once I got in school, that changed. Grand-dad would invite me to stay with him. At that time, he lived in Stratton. At first it was a weekend now and then, but as I got older, I spent entire summers at his house.

"He'd bring me out to explore the hills. And he taught me to really see God's green earth. Not just with my eyes. With my ears and my heart too. I guess at first my love for the hills was really just an extension of my feelings for Grand-dad. They were important to him, so they became important to me."

He paused, watching her run her fingers through her hair in an attempt to tidy it. When her hands were still again, he went on.

"It was the same with the dogs. At first, it seemed they were an awful amount of work for no more return than they brought. A beagle doesn't bring down big bucks and I'd been raised to give big bucks top priority.

"Being with Grand-dad was a total reversal. He taught me about the Creator of the simple, meaningful things in life. He was something solid and unchange-able in my life.

"If he said he'd come to my little league game, then

71

no matter how busy he was, he came. If he said we'd go fishing on Saturday, we went fishing. If he said he'd tan my hide if he caught me smoking with my friends again, then I could count on him meaning it."

He fell silent, and Mandy sat quietly, watching that half-smile of his take shape. The shaft of light from above picked out shallow dimples on each cheek. More creases than dimples, she decided, intrigued by the way they framed his mouth.

His gaze met hers and held, as he added in a quiet voice, "One more thing, Grand-dad taught me, and that was to wait for a special kind of a girl, not to settle for mediocre."

He rose from his elbow to trace the gentle curve of her chin. Her skin tingled from his touch and she caught her breath as his face drew nearer, so near, his features seemed to blur before her starry eyes. She wanted his kiss, wanted it badly, yet in her yearning there was an unexplored element that frightened her too and at the last moment, she drew back.

Over the loud pounding of her own heart, she heard the ragged sound of his sigh. Yet he got to his feet and offered her a hand up as if nothing had happened between them and she was infinitely glad she hadn't let the kiss occur. It seemed so evident to her in that moment that, though it would have changed her world, it would have been just another kiss as kisses go to him.

She'd exchanged kisses like that with Corey and now realized in one enlightened moment, they were shallow and meaningless. So thinking, she vowed it wouldn't happen again. It wasn't fair to Corey. He deserved a girl who felt for him what she felt for this man at her side.

"The rain seems to have let up," T.K. said into the frantic scurry of her thoughts. "Shall we go?"

Mutely, she nodded and took the checkered spread from the cave floor. Before she could fold it, he took it from her and, with a careless fold, tucked it into the hamper.

The trail he chose down from the bluff was far easier than the one they'd scurried up in the rain. Mandy made her own way with little assistance from him. The walk back started out in silence, a silence that made her feel cut off and hurt.

Had she ruined things, drawing back from his kiss? If she had, spoke her common sense loud and clear, then he wasn't the man she thought him to be. Pride stiffened her spine and held back waves of pain. What had he expected? That she'd fall into his arms, an easy conquest? One second he was talking about a special kind of a girl and the next . . . she stopped short. On the path in front of her, T.K. pivoted to face her.

"Did I thank you for sharing your picnic lunch?" he asked, managing to sound very stiff and formal. "If I didn't, I am now."

Mandy's hurt fell away and her tongue loosened. "And I should thank you for sharing your picnic spot, as well as telling me about the cave."

The winking sun filtered through wet branches and leaves, shedding light on the relief in T.K.'s eyes. "I thought I'd either bored you half to death, or frightened you off."

Lowering her lashes, Mandy refused to take his words in the frank way he meant them. "Frightened me?" she said, a bit breathless. "By your tales of ghostly Indians haunting the cave? Come now. I'm made of sterner stuff."

His smile came out like a rainbow. "That's good to know. Then I feel free to ask, would you like to do some honest-to-goodness cave exploring with me a week from Saturday?"

Beaming back at him, she replied, "I'd love to."

"And you'll go on using the lodge as long as you need it?"

Her smile gave way to an anxious expression. "Are you *sure* you don't care?"

In answer, he caught her hand and gave it a squeeze. "I'd care if you *didn't*." Then, looking her over, he said, rather critically she thought, "I hope you have something in your closet besides skirts and sandals. Spelunking's hard on shoe leather, not to mention knees and elbows and . . ."

Laughing, Mandy held up a hand. "Whoa! You'll talk me out of it."

"Too late to back out. You already agreed." Keeping a firm grip on her hand, he began schooling her on cave exploration as they continued on to the lodge.

Mandy listened, while silently exploring the new feelings flowing between them. Like raindrops, the feelings were sparkling, fresh, and delicate too.

As the first tides of love lapped at her heart, she winged a prayer heaven-ward. "Lord, if he isn't feeling what I'm feeling, grant me the wisdom to . . ."

To what? she wondered, and left the prayer unfinished.

CHAPTER 5

BECAUSE LOVE WAS NEW, a week and a day seemed to Mandy a long time. A time in which anything could happen. He might change his mind, his interest might lag, he might even be called out of town.

Foolish worries, Mandy reasoned in her more sane moments. But love seemed to bring out the foolishness in her. As the days passed and her hopes that T.K. would stop by the lodge or call went unfulfilled, her spirits drooped. She'd find her mind wandering like the swallow-tail butterflies that flitted about outside the lodge door. Instead of the flower-girl's dress beneath the pressure-foot of her machine, she'd be calling to memory T.K.'s every feature, his thick-lashed grey eyes, his straight mouth that could turn up in a smile at a second's notice, the tiny scar that ran through his left eyebrow.

Sometimes in the evening, when she dropped by Gram's to help with Ellen's wedding preparations, she'd catch herself mentioning this or that about T.K., just for the pleasure of saying his name aloud.

And worse yet, when Kyle stopped by the lodge for

a visit, she'd hang on his every word, willing him to mention "the boy," as he fondly called T.K.

Corey called in the middle of the week. Uncomfortable now with the knowledge he wanted far more than the friendship she had to offer, she used Ellen's wedding preparations as an excuse why she could not go out with him.

She hung up moments later, her mind in confusion over how to deal with Corey. She felt there were truths she should be sharing with him—spiritual truths, yet it was so hard for her. Faith had always been such a personal thing, and she was timid about sharing it.

She didn't want to lose him as a friend, yet she'd been hesitant to let him know she was still using the lodge, for fear he'd guess she'd done just what she'd assured him she wouldn't. She'd given T.K. her heart.

Because Ellen wished to hold the wedding reception in the yard at home, weather permitting, Mandy kept busy toward the end of the week helping to get things in shape.

"The weather had better permit, after all the work we're doing," she grumbled as she plucked dry blooms off Gram's petunias.

"Lord willing." Gram wiped sweat from her wrinkled brow.

Ellen bounced around the side of the house, looking as fresh and lovely as Gram's summer roses. "Dad's trimmed the lower branches off the weeping willow. Come see how nice it looks. I think I'll tie yellow bows on the branches. Won't that be pretty?"

She went on and on, but Mandy caught only snatches as she followed her to the back yard. Ellen's boundless enthusiasm for this wedding was a wonder to behold. What would she do with herself when the knot was tied and life resumed a normal pace?

"The hedges still need to be clipped," she was saying, "and I do wish Daddy'd do something about that hanging gutter. Oh, and don't forget, the vegetable garden needs some weeding too."

Mandy cast a look in that direction and sighed. Gram kept a no-fuss garden. She was out for the produce, and stepping around a weed or two to get it didn't bother her much.

"Are you sure you wouldn't like to hold this reception in the church basement?" Mandy suggested. "It's my month to do the janitoring anyway, so it won't put anyone else out."

"Don't be silly, Mand. Now, about the garden," Ellen prattled on.

Wavering between amusement and affectionate irritation, Mandy tuned her out. A while later, she remarked to her father as he set the clippers aside and settled into a lawn chair, "If Ellen doesn't fly into a dozen pieces before this is all over, it'll be a miracle."

"That's the most pessimistic thing I think you've ever said." Her father gave her close scrutiny. "What's wrong with you anyway? You've been moody for two or three days. That isn't like you at all."

Little brown wood nuts didn't get moody? She brushed the thought aside and thread a blade of grass through her fingers. "I'm serious. She's so keyed up, fussing over every single detail. I'm kind of worried. I have the feeling she could burst into tears of hysteria if the least little thing goes wrong."

"Pooh," her father dismissed her concern. "She's having the time of her life. Look at her. She glows like a light-bulb."

It was true. Ellen *did* glow. Mandy shrugged off her worry as Ellen came to join them under the shade tree.

"Mandy, I want you to come with me Saturday to listen to the soloist practice. I'm having trouble deciding on the first song for her to sing. The words of one are very moving. Guaranteed to draw tears! The other, the music is simply inspiring. Maybe you can help me choose between them."

"I can't Saturday, Ellen. I have a date." Mandy rose and brushed the grass from the seat of her shorts.

"Corey'll understand." Ellen swept her excuse aside. "Bring him along if you like. After we've listened to the soloist, he can help us tie up little bags of rice for the reception."

Mandy shook her head. "Sorry, Ellen. You'll have to get by without me Saturday."

"But I *need* you!" Tears pricked Ellen's lovely eyes and Mandy gave her father a meaningful look.

"Tell you what, Ellen. I'll help you with the rice Saturday evening. You can take Gram to the church with you to hear the soloist. Gram has a good ear for music. She'll help you decide."

Gram jumped in to reassure Ellen. The tears evaporated and Mandy went off to the garden wondering if this wedding was really worth all the wear and tear on everyones' nerves.

Taking her worries out on the weeds, she'd demolished a good many of them when her father came, offering a glass of iced tea.

"Did Gram get her calmed down?" Mandy asked, between sips of tea.

"She's chirping like a wren again. You were right, though. How'd I miss it?"

Mandy patted his hand. "She's a woman, Dad. There are a few things I see that aren't so evident to you."

"Maybe you'd care to enlighten me." He favored her with a dry smile.

Stepping into the shade, she took a long drink. "I suppose for all her bluffing to the contrary, she's going through some premarital jitters. It's a big step she's taking, and she isn't stupid. On the outside, she keeps busy ordering flowers, making lists, planning and replanning. But on the inside, she knows it isn't the wedding that has to be successful. It's the marriage.''

He eased out a long sigh. "You think I should have a talk with her?''

Mandy was sorry for him. It was times like this he must really miss her mother. She said, ''There probably are a few things you could say to reassure her. I think she knows what she's doing, mostly. But it's nice to have someone care enough to be concerned anyway.''

He nodded, then took a final drink before dumping his ice cubes on the ground. ''About your date on Saturday. It isn't with Corey, is it?''

''How'd you know?''

He smiled. ''You haven't been yourself all week, and somehow, T.K. Cooke's name keeps getting dropped into the conversation.''

Chuckling at her blush of confirmation, he turned and walked back to the house.

Was she *that* obvious! Shaken, she sat down in the grass, thinking for all the advice she had to offer on Ellen, she wasn't handling her own affairs so smoothly.

Inside, she was feeling uncertain. Loving T.K. had happened so suddenly. Oh, in the stories and movies, it happened that way. But in real life she'd expected love to come slowly, to build from friendship and trust and common interests. Was what she felt for T.K. only a strong physical attraction? There was no denying he could melt her with a look from those arresting grey eyes. And when his hand clasped hers . . .

This is getting me nowhere, she thought, and went back to pulling weeds.

Saturday came at last. Mandy dressed with care in her favorite blue blouse and designer jeans. Taking T.K.'s advice, she chose sturdy waffle-soled shoes instead of sandals. She dabbed on a fragrant perfume, then paused in recapping the bottle, her attention captured by something in her expression. Why, she looked as excited and eager as Ellen had been looking of late!

Lord, give me peace, give me calm, she prayed as the doorbell rang. Catching her first glimpse of him, handsome in casual jeans and a sweatshirt, she caught her breath thinking it seemed a year since the rainy day they'd picnicked.

By an effort, her lips shaped ordinary words. "A sweatshirt? Won't you roast?"

"It's a little warm now," he admitted, "but the cave stays a constant sixty degrees. You'd better grab a sweater. Make it something old—it'll probably never be the same again."

Mandy said, "I'm not sure I like the sound of this. I'll warn you right now, I always came in near the last when we ran the obstacle course in high school gym class. The passing years have changed nothing in that department."

"You never had T.K. Cooke for a teacher."

For some unknown reason, she flushed, and tried to cover by asking, "Shall I pack a picnic lunch?"

"No. Grand-dad's expecting us back at the house for a late lunch. He wants to repay you for all the lunches you've shared with him over the past couple of weeks."

"I've enjoyed his company," Mandy said, ducking into her bedroom to find a sweater.

As she came back with it, he scanned her from head to toe and gave her a vote of approval. "Strap some tire rubber to your knees and you'll pass for a seasoned spelunker."

"Does that mean we're going to have to *crawl?*"

"Only when sneaking past swarming bats."

For one brief moment, she thought of Corey. He too could tease with a perfectly straight face. "I wasn't born yesterday," she informed him, locking her apartment door as they left. "It's bees that swarm, not bats."

"You're sure of that?"

"Yes, and anyway bats snooze during the day."

"Right. In caves."

"Hanging upside down, not swarming on innocent explorers," she said.

He sighed. "Been doing research, huh?"

"No, but I have been to a commercial cave or two." Crossing the parking lot to his waiting car, Mandy added, "And they all have one thing in common. Little plaques that read 'Jesse James Slept Here'."

He arched a serious eyebrow. "You doubt it?"

"I'm no more a skeptic on Jesse James camping out in every cave in Missouri than I am on swarming bats."

"Since you're such an authority on bats," he said, "perhaps you know their droppings are used in making a cosmetic you women are all fond of using."

"I seriously doubt that. Fertilizer, maybe. Cosmetics? I don't think so."

"Really!" he insisted, holding the car door for her. "You could be wearing some now . . . yes, I think you are." He inclined his face, brushing her shoulder. "Perfume. That's it."

"Bat droppings in perfume?" She slid onto the seat. "I don't believe you."

"I'm a reliable source," he insisted, coming around to his side. "Didn't I tell you my mother was in the cosmetic business."

"What'd she specialize in—bat perfume?"

The firm line of his mouth quivered as he fit the key to the ignition, but otherwise, there was no indication whether or not he was teasing.

"What brand did you say this perfume was?"

"There's a fancy French name for it. One that disguises the ingredients."

"Uh-huh. Sure."

"Would I mislead you?" he asked, cruising smoothly through Saturday morning traffic.

"I don't know. Let me check with my friendly neighborhood cosmetologist, then I'll decide."

He laughed and changed the subject. "How's your sewing progressing this week?"

"Fine. All my sewing for Ellen's wedding is finished. How about you?"

"So-so at the factory."

"And the dog farm?"

"The dog farm?" He laughed as he executed a sharp turn in the road. "Is that what you consider Grand-dad and I to be? Dog farmers?"

"Kyle, most definitely. He's very single-minded about his beagles. As for you, you've diversified, it seems. Maybe one of these days, you'll come up with an innovative way to turn house-broken puppies off the assembly line as easily as you do flea-powder and chew bones."

He laughed again and she began to relax. It was getting easier. T.K. picked up on silliness as readily as Corey and could hand it back with a charm she adored.

"I'll work on that idea," he said, "but not today. Today's special. I've been looking forward to it all week."

"Bringing back all those boyhood memories? Playing Tom Sawyer exploring the cave?"

"More than that. Exploring it with you."

Heart taking careless flight, she laced her fingers in her lap and sat back to enjoy the passing countryside. Once to the lodge, they proceeded on foot through the shaded forest. At the fern-curtained opening of the cave, T.K. gave her a flashlight as well as a couple of emergency candles.

Then, carrying a carbide lamp, he lead the way inside. Mandy stayed close behind, intimidated not only by the deep darkness of the cave, but also the awesome quiet.

Thankful T.K. had suggested the sweater, Mandy pushed her arms into it. T.K.'s lamp bobbed ahead of her. Hurrying to catch up she said, "It's kind of spooky isn't it, hearing nothing but your own footsteps? I expected to hear a little wind whistling through the cracks, water trickling, something."

"There isn't any wind today. But we'll get into some water up ahead. And you don't have to whisper. All the murdering outlaws have passed on to their just rewards."

He chuckled, but he reached out to squeeze her hand as if he understood her sudden timidity. "If you want to turn back, we can."

"No, I want to go on. I've always wanted to do this."

"Then duck," he warned, letting go her hand to squeeze through a low passageway. "Grand-dad always called this spot, 'Low Clearance'."

It was only the first of such passageways, and as they made their way through the meandering cave, they came up with names to fit some of the more difficult spots to traverse. 'Gang-buster', 'Excedrin Headache', 'Fat Man's Squeeze'.

Through laughter and complaints alike, Mandy beamed her flashlight into passageways and chambers, finding similarities, yet a uniqueness too about each one.

The cave floor became gummy mud. They waded through a cavern stream, drained their shoes, crawled over an obstructing boulder only to be faced with another watery passage.

"A person could drown in here on a rainy day," Mandy said, tipping the water out of her shoes for a second time.

T.K. sat on the rock beside her, emptying his own boots. "Ready to see some mineral formations?"

"Stalactites and stalagmites? Really?"

"Maybe not like those you see at the commercial caves," he cautioned. "These are babies by comparison. But interesting all the same."

Her weariness erased by a readiness to cram all they could see into one morning, Mandy tied her shoes, reached for her light and bounded off the rock. "Let's go."

They trudged on, eventually arriving at a room which was fifteen or so feet high. Taking a flashlight from his pocket, T.K. set the carbide lamp aside. Urging Mandy to follow suit, he shone the light on the cave ceiling.

"They are baby stalactites!" Mandy cried, her light picking out the slender crystalline formations. "They look like colored icicles, don't they?"

"They're called soda-straw stalactites," T.K. told her. "Most of them are still forming. See the tiny single droplets clinging to the tip of them?"

After pointing out another knobby growth on the wall—cave popcorn—he called it, T.K. lead the way to the cave's own small lake. In actuality, it was a shallow depression in the cave floor. A small stream ran into it and was trapped there.

Shining the lantern over the water, T.K. pointed with the flashlight he held in his other hand. Mandy squatted next to the pool of water, intrigued by the colorless fish not much larger than a goldfish, staying quite still near the bottom.

Because they were blind, they reacted not at all to the light. But when T.K. dropped a small pebble in the water, they darted about.

"They sense the motion of the water," T.K. explained. "Like a sightless person, they compensate with other senses being highly developed. Speaking of which," he went on, "did you ever stop to wonder what it would be like to be blind?"

Without awaiting her reply, he turned out the lantern and switched off his flashlight.

Mandy scrambled to her feet, clinging to her own flashlight.

"Turn it off," he urged. "You won't believe how really dark it is."

None too keen on the idea, but unwilling to seem a spoil-sport, Mandy switched off her flashlight and plunged the cave into immediate blackness. The darkness was overwhelming. She waved her hand in front of her face, but saw nothing. It was like being shut in a vast empty space all alone. Knowing T.K. to be right beside her did not ward off the uneasy feeling of disorientation. She stepped closer, her head brushing his shoulder.

"Spooky, isn't it?" His voice echoed through the empty chambers.

"Poor fish," she murmured, reaching for his hand.

"I don't know, they manage to survive."

"On what?" she asked.

"Bat perfume." He chuckled as he drew her to himself.

His heart-beat was a heavy knock against her ear as his arms tightened in a lover's hold.

"The dark isn't so bad if you have someone to hold on to," he said, his voice a low rumble nearly lost to the thunder in her ears.

"No," she whispered back, for in his arms, there was no darkness or light, only him.

His hand crept up her back and lost itself in the silky texture of her hair. "You're beautiful, Mandy."

She nestled her face against the soft fabric of his sweatshirt and murmured, "A fine compliment coming from a man in the dark."

"Not just on the outside," he went on, ignoring her effort to keep this magic between them on a lighter plane. "But on the inside too, where it really counts."

"You don't know me," she said, half embarrassed by the finesse of his compliment.

"Don't I? Then let me tell you what I see. I see a

girl who runs out in the rain to get cat food for her neighbor's cat. A girl who speaks of her sister and father and grandmother with deep affection. A girl who strikes up a friendship with a lonesome old man, in spite of his shadow, the dog. Now don't tell me I don't know you.''

His arms tightened around her as he trailed slow-burning kisses down her hairline.

It was dangerous, being so lost to his touch.

"Let's go," she whispered. "Turn on the lantern.''

"When you've kissed me.''

Heart racing, she turned her head. His lips brushed her cheek.

"Mandy?'' He questioned so much, just saying her name.

Quick tears stung her eyes. "I'm afraid.''

"Afraid of me?''

"No. Afraid of loving you,'' the truth slipped out, surprising them both. She tried to break free, but he was no longer asking. His mouth found hers in a kiss so deep and true, she no longer wanted to be free, only to be kissed by him forever. For a time, it seemed her wish would be, for he had taken leisurely possession of her mouth, his desire heightened by her response. His lips found the throbbing pulse at the base of her throat, touching off a delicious free-floating sensation before moving back to her mouth.

In the end, it was he who broke away and reached for the lantern. When it flared, lighting his face, he looked shaken from that perpetual calm of his.

"No wonder you were afraid.''

His words were softly spoken. She could have misunderstood his meaning, but she thought not. It was as if he'd put her heart under a microscope, then stepped away, put off at what he'd seen. Even in the cool of the cave, her face felt fiery hot. She'd spilled her true feelings, held nothing in reserve, not even a bit of pride to fall back on.

She turned and followed him out, no longer caring if she ever saw the light of day. How was she going to face him? He knew her heart as well as she knew it herself. And he didn't want what she had to offer. He'd only wanted a few meaningless kisses in a dank and creepy old cave.

She shivered and wiped a cobweb out of her face. The magic was gone.

CHAPTER 6

"IT'S ONE-THIRTY. GRAND-DAD'S going to give up on us." T.K. stowed the carbide lamp and the flashlights in the trunk of his car before opening the passenger door for Mandy.

"Don't worry about the car," he said, when she tossed the soiled sweater on the floor and brushed off her jeans. "Let's get going. I'm starved."

His jeans as damp and soiled as hers, he climbed behind the wheel and turned the car around. Heading back out over the primitive bridge, he asked, "So what'd you think? Did it live up to all your expectations?"

Thoughts steeped in humiliation—how *could* she have kissed him like that?—Mandy misinterpreted his question. Her face flashed hot, but she tipped her chin to a haughty angle and replied, "I've been kissed before."

Grey gaze sweeping her burning face, he chuckled. "So I gathered. But I wasn't thinking of that. I meant *the cave*. Did you like it?"

Why didn't she just wait until he got the car up to

forty or so and jump out? It probably wouldn't surprise him. She'd been such an idiot thus far.

"Did you?" he prompted.

Badly as she wished to reestablish that ease that had been between them before that soul-revealing interlude in the cave, it was hard. Striving for a normal tone, she said, "Yes, the cave was interesting. A lot bigger than I imagined, too."

And so is love, she thought, stealing a glimpse of his face. Eyes on the road, he looked very secure in a roguish sort of way. And why wouldn't he? She was the one writhing in insecurities, sinking deeper and deeper in love with a guy who considered her a casual date, a stolen kiss, someone to hook on a smooth age-old line.

"You're beautiful Mandy, on the inside too." How could she have fallen for that? How could she have fallen for him at all? Corey had warned her the man left a trail of broken hearts. And she'd tossed his warning to the wind. Laughed even, as if it could never happen to her.

I should have listened to Corey, she thought, as they completed the short drive. Now she would have to teach herself to forget this man.

As the car purred up a twisting, tree-shrouded lane, Mandy stirred from her thoughts. The trees were trimmed back from the road in a tidy row. The grass was clipped and the road itself was well kept. Even then, Mandy was ill-prepared for the dignified mansion just beyond yawning rod-iron gates.

Taking in the capacious three-story Victorian structure in one sweeping glance, Mandy exclaimed, "What a beautiful home!"

T.K. grinned as he took a circular drive to the rear of the house. "Not bad for a dog farm, eh?"

Trying to hide her discomfort over ill-chosen words, Mandy scanned the shady lawn, the colorful flower-beds and the huge old trees as T.K. braked to a stop. She asked, "Where do you keep the dogs?"

"Down the hill. I'll show you after lunch, if you'd like."

"No, no," Mandy assured him of her disinterest in a hurry. "I was just curious, that's all."

T.K. grinned again. "Grand-dad would like them closer to the house, but Mrs. Hart put her foot down. She can't abide a dog in or anywhere near the house."

"Who is Mrs. Hart?" Mandy asked, as with a guiding hand on her elbow, he lead her on a path that skirted around the house to the front entrance.

"She's our live-in housekeeper. I guess you could say she came with the house."

"Kyle's never mentioned her. I was under the impression he was on his own for the weeks you were gone."

Eyes warm with affection, T.K. said, "Grand-dad would lead you to believe that. She's a sore subject with him."

"Why is that?"

"Partly because of the dog kennels. They injure Mrs. Hart's dignity beyond repair, so she's very uppity with Grand-dad." Mouth slanting a smile, he picked one of the many peonies dotting the pathway. Tucking it behind her ear, he arranged her soft curls around it and went on with his explanation.

"To tell you the truth, the pair of them seem to enjoy playing tricks on one another. Really childish." But he laughed like he found it rather entertaining.

Enthralled in spite of herself, Mandy asked, "What sort of tricks?"

"Grand-dad's favorite is letting Clancy in the house on Mrs. Hart's days off. The next day, when she finds dog hair here and there, she retaliates by misplacing something dear to Grand-dad's heart. His favorite walking stick, his old hat. Right now, his pocketknife is missing."

Stone steps worn smooth from the traffic of generations lead up to a veranda which spanned the entire

90

front side of the house. To the left, as they climbed the steps, the veranda was screened in. To their right, it was open and continued on around to the south side of the house. A huge door, ornate with wood carving opened and Kyle greeted them with his wrinkled grin.

"Thought I was going to have to send out a search party. You two get lost, did you?"

As he stepped aside and let them enter the wide hall, Mandy looked around, eyes drinking in the grandeur of another era. High-ceilinged rooms split off from the spacious hallway in an intriguing fashion and she yearned to explore.

Noting her interest, Kyle said, "T.K. will show you around after lunch. Mrs. Hart's fuming from being kept waiting. One o'clock is her sacred lunch hour. You're late."

"We're going to risk her good humor a minute longer." T.K. gestured toward the staircase. "Show Mandy upstairs so she can wash up."

Mandy climbed the carpeted stairway behind Kyle, glad for the opportunity to make herself a bit more presentable. After washing her hands and face, she combed her hair and resecured the fragrant deep-red peony in her shining tresses.

Satisfied her reflection betrayed none of the bewilderment she was feeling at the realization T.K. lived and took for granted a lifestyle far removed from hers, Mandy followed Kyle down the stairs and into the dining room.

Boasting a table that would easily seat sixteen, a sideboard that rose to the ceiling, and a gorgeous gold-leaf framed mirror, the dining room was impressive.

A tempting salad luncheon was spread atop a delicately hand-crocheted white tablecloth. The china settings seemed unnecessarily formal for the occasion.

But, as Mrs. Hart came into the room to pour the

cold drinks, Mandy saw right away she wasn't the sort of housekeeper to consider the kitchen a proper setting for the most informal of luncheons.

T.K. made introductions, adding, "Mrs. Hart worked for my grandparents, who lived in the house for many years. My mother's parents, that is," he clarified. "After their death, she cared for the house. Her knowledge of the place is much greater than mine Mandy, so if you're wanting to look around, I'm sure she would be glad to accompany you."

"I'd be pleased," Mrs. Hart said, though any pleasure she was feeling was well guarded behind unsmiling features.

"It is such a lovely old house," Mandy felt compelled to say. "I'm interested in hearing its history."

"Then you'll have to hear it from me," the housekeeper said, tossing T.K. a look of disdain. "Thomas, like his mother, has never shown much interest in the house or its history."

Shocked into silence, Mandy glanced first at T.K., then Kyle. Neither looked surprised by the housekeeper's remark. However, when Mrs. Hart made an unhurried exit, Kyle muttered,

"Outspoken old buzzard, isn't she?"

"Behave yourself, Grand-dad," T.K. reproved him mildly.

"What about *her?* You'd think *she* owned the house and *you* were the hired help. She's lived here alone too many years. I think she's touched in the head."

T.K. helped himself to a luscious fruit salad and passed it on. "Not at all, Grand-dad. She's simply never forgiven mother for never showing any interest in her ancestral home. Having none herself, Mrs. Hart is very big on ancestors. Then I inherit the house and suggest a little modernization and naturally, she gets prickly. To her, I'm an interloper.

"Have a roll, Mandy. They're out of this world," he smoothly changed the subject.

Kyle wasn't that easily deterred. "Myself, I'd get shed of that woman. She's too high-handed for my liking. And she hates dogs. Never trust a woman who hates dogs."

T.K.'s dancing gaze swept Mandy. "Careful, Grand-dad. Mandy's not too crazy about dogs either. You surely don't find her unworthy of trust."

Kyle blustered, "Mandy doesn't hate any of God's creatures. She's afraid and that's another matter entirely."

Wishing they'd leave her out of it, Mandy launched into an account of their cave exploration. T.K. joined in and soon Kyle stopped grumbling over Mrs. Hart in favor of relating a few bone chilling cave tales that the hill people passed down from generation to generation.

When they had finished lunch, Mrs. Hart reappeared to whisk away the dishes. Mandy complimented her on the excellence of the meal.

A touch of a smile lightened her severity. "I enjoy cooking for company," she said. "Time was, I'd cook for ten, twelve, sixteen people and think nothing of it. That was when Thomas' mother was growing up here in this house. Sociable she was, bringing in young people all the time."

"I'm sure you were a great help, Mrs. Hart," Mandy said.

"Just let me take these dishes to the kitchen, and I'll show you around the house," the housekeeper said.

"I'd be glad to help . . ." Mandy began, but Mrs. Hart cut her short.

"No, that wouldn't do at all. Thomas, take the young lady into the parlor. I'll be there directly."

Obedient to Mrs. Hart, T.K. lead the way into the parlor. Kyle followed close behind, grumbling about his missing pocketknife.

T.K. chuckled. "Mrs. Hart seems to be warming up

to Mandy. Maybe *she* can get her to tell what she's done with your knife.''

''Terrible thing when a man can't even lay his pocketknife down.'' Kyle settled onto a camelback sofa.

''Maybe you just mislaid it,'' Mandy suggested for the sake of peace.

''Yes, and maybe he didn't have Clancy in the house yesterday,'' T.K. said with meaning.

Kyle got up and left them, muttering something about a man's home supposed to be his castle. T.K. laughed.

''Don't let him fool you. He wouldn't put Mrs. Hart out on the street anymore than I would. I suspect deep down, when he isn't irked over all her proper ways, he rather admires her.''

''You aren't suggesting he's . . .''

''Sweet on her?'' T.K. finished. ''Could be. Which probably makes him feel foolish, so he tries to convince himself Mrs. Hart is no more than an annoying old lady.''

''But why would being fond of her make him feel foolish?'' Mandy lifted thick, dark lashes in a questioning glance. ''Because of his age?''

''Age has nothing to do with it.'' T.K. met her gaze steadily. ''Being attracted to a lady makes a man vulnerable. Vulnerable and foolish are hard to tell apart. We men get them confused all the time.''

Women too, Mandy thought, heart turning over as he reached out to touch the flower in her hair. How effortlessly he set her senses soaring! And how easy it would be to lose herself in his arms, forgetting for a while that attraction wasn't enough, that attractions fade, leaving a wounded heart behind.

His hand slid down to cup her chin. As his face drew near to hers she whispered his name on a shattered breath, ''T.K., don't.''

''Why?'' His eyes made an unhurried exploration of her troubled, love-soft features.

She did not reply. His lips brushed hers teasingly, but she held herself rigid and unresponsive. A questioning frown tugged at his mouth, but before he could put any words to it, Mrs. Hart came into the parlor.

"Are you ready to see the house, Miss Holt?" she asked.

Thankful for the interruption, Mandy turned away from T.K. and his intoxicating grey eyes. Her heart was in such turmoil, it was difficult to keep her mind on what the housekeeper was saying as she lead her through the house.

The impressive old mansion had been in T.K.'s mother's family for five generations. A pioneering forefather had built and furnished it from wealth he'd amassed mining lead and iron when less patient men had moved on in search for gold.

There was a museum quality about the old house, it seemed to Mandy as Mrs. Hart pointed out the Victorian architecture, the cornices rising over lace-curtained windows, the furnishings of rosewood and walnut.

The theme upstairs was the same. Huge bedrooms housed massive and elaborately carved beds and dressers topped by marble. The floorboards creaked beneath the carpets, a reminder that age did take its toll. Mandy thoroughly enjoyed the tour, as well as Mrs. Hart's shared knowledge of the history of the different furnishings.

Later, on the ride home, Mandy remarked to T.K., "You must be very proud to live in a house that stands as a monument to your ancestors' achievements."

Puzzling over his lack of interest in the house, Mandy was silent the remainder of the ride home. When he parked in the lot behind her building, she watched afternoon sunlight play across his face. It was a face she could have studied forever and been none the wiser. He gave so little away.

"I had a nice day," he said, his voice seeming muted by traffic passing on a side street. "Did you?"

Sorry the day had ended, but having a difficult time with words when his eyes were so full of watching, Mandy said, "I loved the house. The cave was fun too."

His eyes crinkled teasingly. "It was, wasn't it? Especially the dark room."

She didn't have to ask which room he meant by that. The laughter upon his face was explanation enough. His gaze altered then, and she turned sharply away from its sudden intimacy and reached for the door handle.

Catching up with her easily, he linked a hand in hers. Burned by his touched, Mandy quickened her steps and drew her hand away at her door.

"I did have a nice time. Thank you, T.K."

Taking the door key from her unsteady hand, T.K. gently mocked her words. "'I had a nice time, thank you and good-bye.' Come on, Mandy. What gives here?"

"I don't know what you mean." Mandy reached out to turn the door knob, but his hand covered hers in a stopping motion.

"One minute you're warm and friendly, the next it's as if an icy wind has blown through. I feel like I've been on a roller coaster ride spanning the north and south pole. Just tell me where I stand. Do you like me or don't you?"

Backed into a corner by his bluntness, Mandy risked exposing her headstrong heart and admitted, "Of course I like you. You're attentive and handsome and charming . . ."

". . . and you trust me about as far as you trust poor Clancy," he finished for her and laughed softly at her reaction.

Blushing hot with the knowledge it was her own emotions she mistrusted more than him, Mandy tried to think how to squeeze out of this conversation without betraying herself completely. Dear Lord, why hadn't someone warned her it would be this difficult?

"I don't mistrust you," she said finally, lowering her lashes lest her eyes mirror her inward turmoil.

"Good." He smiled a pleased smile. "Now that that's settled, let's make some future plans. Have you ever been to Branson?"

"No," Mandy said, though it was a place she'd always meant to go.

"There is a lot to do there. Country music shows, an outdoor theatre, Silver Dollar City, good restaurants and a lot of interesting shops."

Begin to forget him? Already her traitorous heart was clamoring for another chance to be with him. "It sounds like fun, but I've so much to do," Mandy wavered. "Ellen's wedding is just around the corner, and . . ."

"No excuses." A blunt-tipped finger reached out to silence her lips and send a tingling sensation down her spine. "Ellen can worry about her own wedding. As for work, we've all week to work. The weekend is for relaxation.

"We could drive to Branson Friday afternoon and see the play that evening after dinner. Then on Saturday, we'll do Silver Dollar City. Sunday afternoon, we could take a boat out on the lake. Or go shopping. Whatever you would enjoy. So what do you say?"

Her mind tumbled into a panicky deep-freeze, while he awaited her reply. Why, he was inviting her to spend a weekend with him! And doing it as casually as he'd ask for a dinner date! Did he assume, because they'd shared a few kisses, she'd go anywhere, do anything? Was *that* his opinion of her?

Head lowered to conceal the hurt and confusion she felt, Mandy murmured, "No thank-you, T.K."

Before his surprise could give way to questions, she

bid him good-afternoon and slipped into her apartment to listen as his footsteps faded down the hallway.

Out of her life. A tear hovered on her eyelashes. If he was the sort of man who thought she'd have no qualms about spending the weekend with him, why should she care he was walking out of her life?

The why of it was unfathomable, but the tears were very real. She dashed at them with tight fists. How dare he, anyway? It was one thing for him to have kissed her into spilling her heart in return kisses, then to have appeared startled by the depth of her emotion and backing off to safety. That, at least, was an honest reaction. He hadn't felt what she'd felt, and he'd made no pretense of returning her love.

But this! This was as if he'd decided to cash in on those feelings of hers. Beneath the anger, there was a bittersweet sadness that made her feel old and weary.

She stripped out of her clothes and stood under the shower, letting the steaming water wash away her tears. Overexerted muscles began to relax, and gradually she became calmer. If only sore hearts could be cured so easily.

It seemed she'd no more than towel-dried when the phone began to ring. It was Ellen, reminding her of her promise to help cut out with netting and ribbon for the little rice packets.

Saying she'd be right over, Mandy hung up the phone. It was good she wouldn't have to spend a lonely evening at home with nothing for company but downward spiraling dreams.

Because it seemed unthinkable that she remain at the lodge after all that had transpired, Mandy drove out Sunday afternoon and emptied it of every trace of her short occupancy. Waves of sadness engulfed her as she locked the door for the last time and put the key beneath the mat.

Walking up the hill, she gazed at the beauty all

around her, thinking of a verse she'd memorized as a child. "I will lift up mine eyes unto the hills, from whence cometh my strength." Like a balm to her sore heart, she said the verse over, being reminded of the source of all love.

God's love was tender and compassionate, all knowing, all seeing, all caring. Even when all else failed, He was there to comfort, guard, guide and direct.

She released a long sigh. The light breeze carried the sound of it away and she resolved to let the hurt go in like manner.

Easier said than done, for no matter how many times during the next week Mandy gave the disappointment and pain up to God, it came back like a faithful homing pigeon.

Work helped. She sewed with such single-minded determination, when night came she fell into bed one exhausted heap and slept a dreamless sleep. But in the morning, as he day began, renegade thoughts wandered in and she'd find herself dwelling upon the way T.K.'s high, prominent cheekbones had first reminded her of a proud Indian warrior. Or how the fine, straight line of his mouth could twist into a smile. Great flames of longing would burn deep in her heart. This pain called love, she'd pray, God, deliver me.

Just as her sewing demands helped, so did Ellen's needs. Ellen—her face wreathed in smiles one moment, then terribly distraught the next over some minor cog in the wedding plans.

"Everything is going to be just fine," Mandy assured her sister on Monday when Ellen came to her apartment all in a stew because the florist was afraid she wouldn't be able to come up with any lilies-of-the-valley for the bridesmaids' bouquets. "She'll substitute something just as lovely. Ellen, you have to relax, or by June twenty-seventh, there'll be nothing left of you but a bundle of nerves."

"I wish it was over and done with and Gregory and I were on our honeymoon. That's what I wish!" Ellen fidgeted with Mandy's sewing scissors.

Taking them from her, Mandy said, "Don't wish it away, Ellen. You've planned for months and months. It's a day you'll remember the rest of your life. Everything is going to go smooth as silk."

It was a pep speech she repeated on Tuesday and Wednesday. On Thursday, she did a familiar version of it and still Ellen seemed to be tightly coiled.

Thursday evening, after doing her weekly cleaning at the church, Mandy's worst fears were realized. She'd gone to the jewelers with Ellen to pick up Gregory's wedding band. It had been selected well ahead of time and left to be engraved with the couples' initials, as well as their wedding date, on the inside of the wide band.

Ellen's eager pink-tipped fingers took the velvet lined box from the jeweler and worked it open. "Isn't it pretty?" All dimples, she flashed the ring under Mandy's nose.

"Lovely," Mandy said, though it differed very little from any other plain gold band.

"And the initials are in script," Ellen went on, turning the band up to the light. Like city lights in a black-out, her smile plunged into darkness. "Oh, no!"

Her wail made both Mandy and the on-looking jeweler jump. Mystified, they watched her tick off the months on her fingers.

"January, February, March, April, May, June. June is the sixth month! Not the seventh! Mandy, look! It reads *7-27-85*. I knew it, I just knew it! And here it is, just eight days until our wedding. What am I going to do?"

"This isn't right," she said to the jeweler, and shoved it back over the counter. "I don't believe this is happening to me."

"Shh!" Mandy admonished her gently. "It isn't that big of a deal."

"Isn't a big deal? Would you want your husband's wedding band to read the wrong date? What's the point of having the date if it isn't even the right date!" she blew up in Mandy's face.

"Ellen, calm down," Mandy pleaded. "I'm sure we can work something out." To the jeweler, she made her appeal. "You can fix it, can't you?"

He looked up from a nervous shuffling of papers. "One moment. I'm checking out the order." A look of relief crossed his face. "Here's the work sheet. It was engraved the way it was written down."

Mandy looked on while Ellen read the sheet. *7-27-85* was printed in Ellen's script. Ellen burst into tears.

"How could I do anything so stupid? Where was my head? Look at this, Mandy. It was *my* mistake!"

A big tear splashed on the glass counter. Looking grieved and hugely discomfited, the jeweler offered Ellen a tissue saying, "I'll fix it, young woman. I'll fix it tonight, if you'd like. And don't worry, I'll do such a good job, no one will ever guess it didn't read right the first time. Just write it down how you want it, and then stop by in the morning. I'll have it waiting. Will that do?"

Ellen was past pulling herself together. Mandy wrote down the inscription as it should read, thanked the man graciously and hustled Ellen out of the shop. Ellen cried as if she'd never stop. No amount of comforting words could stem the flow of her tears.

In final desperation, Mandy drove her to her apartment, fixed her a cup of tea and changed tactics. Hands cocked on slender hips, she issued an order.

"You stop that crying and drink this tea, Ellen. You're all in a dither over nothing. The man said he'd fix it, for heaven's sake!"

Unaccustomed to harshness in Mandy, Ellen jerked her head up and blinked tear-bleary eyes. "It i-i-isn't the r-ring. It's everything," she stammered.

"I know that." Mandy's tone mellowed. "You have the jitters and who could blame you."

"You're bl-blaming me. You're ye-yelling at me."

"I am not yelling. I'm trying to reason with you. You cannot go on like this. If there is something terribly wrong between you and Gregory, you'd best tell me about it."

"What c-could be wrong with Gregory and me?" Ellen looked shocked at the very idea.

A profound relief washed over Mandy. "Then you aren't having second thoughts?"

"No. How silly do you think I am? When a girl is in love with the man of her dreams, how could she have second thoughts?"

"You're the authority, you tell me," Mandy said with a sharp stab of pain. "Everything is fine with Gregory?"

"Yes."

"And you still get along well with his parents?"

"Yes."

"And you're ready to take on a wife's full role—in every respect?"

"Yes!"

"Then what on earth is wrong with you?"

"You're ye-yelling again," Ellen sniffed.

Mandy did a silent ten count and tried again. Putting a comforting arm around her sister's shoulders, she said, "I'm out of guesses, Ellen. You're going to have to tell me."

"It's just that it's the end of so much. Like high school graduation, but more serious. Know what I mean?"

"You mean you're feeling sad about late cups of cocoa with Gram and Dad, filling them in on your dates? Teasing Dad out of the car? Making strawberry jam with Gram? Things like that?"

Bleary eyes blinking surprise, Ellen asked, "How'd you know?"

Finally understanding, Mandy smiled. "Because I went through the same thing when I got my own

102

apartment. Sometimes I'd go home in the middle of the day, just to see what Gram was cooking for lunch, or if Dad had remembered to put the garbage cans around front on collection day.''

"And you got over it?" Ellen studied her with anxious, tearful eyes.

"Let's say I grew into a life of my own. That doesn't mean you and Dad and Gram are any less a part of my life, though. You know that. And, after you're married, we'll all still be a part of your life. Of course with you, Gregory will come first. But that still leaves plenty of room for the rest of us, doesn't it?"

Ellen nodded. She dashed at her tears. "I'm being childish, aren't I?"

Mandy gave her a hug. "Not at all. I think you've just been worrying about this wedding and keeping things penned inside until the dam burst. You know what you and Gregory need to do is take a day off. Go for a long walk in the hills, take a picnic or something and make it against the rules to say one word about the wedding.''

Ellen blinked and tried a shaky smile. "You're the one who loves the hills. But Gregory and I would comment how lovely the scenery was for about half an hour, then begin to yawn and fidget.''

"Do something else then," Mandy said. "Get away from this wedding business. Empty your mind of it. What do you think?''

"I think it's a good suggestion," Ellen said. She flitted into the bathroom, calling back, "Maybe I'll phone Gregory and suggest it.''

Moments later, Ellen reappeared, nothing but tell-tale red-rimmed eyes to hint at her momentary breakdown. She stopped with her hand on the door and came back to kiss Mandy's cheek.

"In case I've never told you before, I love you, Mandy.''

Ellen breezed out, leaving her to deal with the

103

sentimental lump in her throat. Dear funny Ellen. Taking the empty tea cup to the sink, she prayed Gregory realized her sister's worth and would always be patient and loving.

The phone rang. Hoping it wasn't Corey, for she didn't feel up to coping with him at the moment, Mandy reached for it. Miss Princeton's voice flooded the line.

"I hate to bother you dear, but Willie is missing. He followed me down to the basement storage area earlier today and I don't remember him coming back up. He likes to prowl, you know. Now, I'm afraid he's trapped somewhere down there. I've called and called and he doesn't come."

"I'll go take a look, Miss Princeton," Mandy assured her, accepted her gratitude and returned the phone to the cradle. She'd no more than lifted her hand when it rang again.

"You took your things out of the lodge," accused a voice that went over her like long, languid hours in the sun, driving out all thought of Miss Princeton or her cat Willie.

"T.K.," she murmured his name.

"Why'd you move out?" he demanded.

"It was time," she said, caught off guard by his abrupt tone. "Ellen's wedding is next weekend. Someone has to be here to hold her together."

"Does your sister know what a convenient excuse she makes for you?" he baited.

"That isn't fair, T.K. Ellen's been very high strung lately. You're judging without knowing a thing about the situation."

"You never judge, I suppose."

Stung by his low, tight tone, Mandy retorted, "Not that I'm aware of, no."

"Then I'll make you aware of it," came his terse reply. "You've been judging me since the first time we met. I was okay in your book when I got you past

104

the German shepherd. So I offer you a ride home. You climbed in willingly enough, but then you fixed those mistrustful brown eyes of yours on me, as if you thought I might . . ."

"I didn't know you," she interrupted, face flaming. "In this day and age, a girl *has* to be careful."

"I suppose." He gave her that much. "But you know me now. Have I ever behaved toward you in any way even vaguely improper?"

Not in deed maybe. She clutched the phone tighter. "T.K., what's the point of this?"

"The point is, I haven't. I'd pass Mrs. Hart's high standards of propriety with flying colors. Which hasn't always been easy," he added with a hint of malice.

"I suppose that's my fault," Mandy was needled into retorting.

"Yes, it's your fault. It was you who reached for my hand in the dark of the cave."

"It was *you* who turned off the lantern and flashes. A cheap trick if every I saw it!"

"It was you who brought up love, you who kissed me like you never wanted to stop, you who seemed bewildered when I did stop," he plunged ruthlessly on.

"If you're wanting me to thank you for all that admirable control," Mandy began abruptly, but was cut short.

"I don't want your thanks for anything!" he hissed. "What I would like is to know why you've been running hot and cold ever since. You say you had a nice time, you liked the house, you enjoyed the cave, you even adore my grandfather, but when I asked you out again, I got a point-blank, 'No!' No explanation.

"Now, I'm left wondering are you punishing me for kissing you in the first place, or for stopping when I did?"

Whatever else he had to say, he said to a dead line.

CHAPTER 7

ALMOST AS SOON AS Mandy removed her hand from the phone, it began ringing again. If it had been a ravenous lion, she couldn't have backed away any faster. No way was she going to answer it and risk another explosive exchange with him!

Slipping off her shoes, Mandy sank down on the sofa and tucked her feet beneath her. Soon she would go help Miss Princeton with her cat, but first she needed a moment alone to think things through. The phone finally stopped ringing, but the hurt and humiliation T.K. had inflicted seemed to go deeper the longer she dwelled upon it.

Tears were threatening, but she held them back, thinking how her father always said to try to look at a situation from the other fellow's point of view.

But how could she? "A good name is to be more desired than great riches." How often had Gram quoted her that verse? And she wanted to keep her name clean, to feel free of guilt inside! She could not go against her conscience. Spend a weekend with a man as if it didn't matter. It did matter! It was her choice, and T.K. had no right to be angry because she'd turned him down. So if that was the source of his anger, then why was she suffering over it? He simply wasn't the man she'd hoped him to be.

The doorbell summoned her from her troubled thoughts. Oh dear. Miss Princeton must think she'd forgotten, thought Mandy, coming to her feet.

As she swung the door open, an involuntary gasp left her lips. It was T.K. in the corridor, eyes blazing, hair tossed as if he'd driven willy-nilly with the windows down, mouth drawn out in a ominous line.

"You hung up on me!" he accused.

"Yes, which should have been a very broad hint I wasn't interested in talking any longer," Mandy hid throbbing panic behind a frigid tone, and would have closed the door in his face but that he was too quick. The door rebounded off the toe of his shoe.

"Well *I am,* and you darn well better listen." He stepped in to tower over her as he gave the door a careless fling shut.

"I almost didn't come, just like I *almost* didn't call and I almost refused to think of you all week long," he said tersely. "You're making me crazy, Mandy. And crazy isn't something I enjoy. Now, I want to know what is going on in that head of yours, and I want to know now."

While he ran a brown hand through unruly dark hair, Mandy tilted her chin to a defiant angle and shot back, "*You* want to know, *you* don't enjoy, *you* want to talk. That's it in a nutshell, T.K. It all centers around you. How *you* feel, what *you* want. What about how *I* feel? Doesn't that count for anything?"

A muscle tensed along his clean jawline. He exploded, "Good heavens woman! What does it take to get through to you? That's what I'm asking. Tell me how you feel!"

She ducked her hand to hide the quiver of her chin. "I feel like I'd appreciate a little privacy. You can go any time now."

"I'm not going anywhere. You haven't told me a thing."

"Very well, then *I'll* go." Miss Princeton's expecting me anyway." Head held high, she tried to brush past him.

Catching her wrists, he stepped between her and the door. His voice a quiet warning, he stated, "Game's over, Mandy. You have ten seconds to tell me why you're being so impossible."

"I don't have to tell you anything!" She tried to jerk loose, but his grip tightened and his voice became very clinical.

"No," he said, "but if you don't, I'll come up with a more creative way of getting it out of you."

"Let go of me, T.K.," she said, her voice as unsteady as her fluttering pulse.

"Eight, seven . . ."

"I mean it, let go!" her voice rose in panic as his hands drew her closer.

"Six five, four . . ."

"I'll scream!"

"Two, one. You'd better start screaming." Eyes darkening, he released her wrists, then caught her neatly around the waist to hold her so close her heart leapt out of control and throbbed in every corner of her being.

"This, if I'm not mistaken, is where all the trouble began." He punctuated his words with a wintry smile. "Remember? We were getting along beautifully until I kissed you. Then you kissed me back and betrayed more than you wanted me to know. You women want to be so secretive about what it is you're feeling. Isn't that right? Isn't that what this game of hot and cold is all about?"

His lips found a sensitive ear lobe. "So tell me," he said huskily, "what are you feeling now?"

She held herself rigid, her fists small tight balls pushing against his chest as she tried to cool the fire in

108

her veins. "Let me go," she whispered again, her words thick upon her tongue.

"Not until you tell me why you decided to shut me out of your life. Kisses don't lie, Mandy. Saturday, when we kissed, it was as if it meant something, as if you really cared. I couldn't have been wrong about that."

His mouth was so close, she could feel the warmth of his breath on her face. In a bare whisper, she opened herself up to fresh sorrow. "You weren't. It did mean something to me, something very precious."

"Then why are you suddenly slamming doors in my face?"

"Because we're so different." Eyes swimming, she hid her face in the fabric of his shirt. "I'm an ordinary girl, T.K. I don't have any Cinderella dreams. I want an ordinary sort of guy, a relationship of friendship and trust out of which love can grow."

"And can't we have that?" He tipped her chin up so that it was impossible for her to avoid eye contact.

Sadly, she shook her head. "I don't think so. You aren't ordinary, T.K. I guess all along I've known that. But Saturday, when I saw your home, how you live, and realized just how different we really are . . ."

"Money?" he interrupted, voice shrewd. "That's the excuse you're going to try and hand me? Don't bother. It won't wash. It isn't money standing between us."

"Money's just part of it." Grateful he'd released her chin, she fastened her gaze on the button-hole of his shirt. Reaching out with her hand to touch it, to touch him, she murmured, "It's the kind of man you are. The kind of life you lead. Corey told me the women fall at your feet and I've no reason to doubt it. It would be foolish of me to think what passed between us in the cave that day was new to you. But it *was* new to me. Maybe it's the newness that makes me afraid I can't handle it."

Voice quizzical, he asked, "Handle what?"

"The feelings, T.K."

Though she'd spoken the truth so low, he'd had to incline his head to catch her words, he seemed to understand her meaning, for he held her face between strong brown hands and kissed her very gently before saying, "Then let me handle them."

"Your way of handling them won't work with me," she objected. "I can't just let the feelings take over and run with them. Wherever they might lead me. Unfashionable it may be, but I still cling to the belief some things are sacred."

"And I don't?" he challenged. Thumbs pressing into her cheeks, softly caressing, he kissed her again. "You forget, Grand-dad has been a guiding influence in my life. Trust me, Mandy. I understand what you're saying and I promise, I'll handle it."

"If going off to Brandon for the weekend is your way of handling it," she flared up like a match, "then it seems to me you don't understand what I'm saying at all. I want what there is between us to stay pure and clean. I don't want to get hurt. But if I do, I can stand it, as long as I don't walk away feeling . . . used," she found the word.

"I wouldn't hurt you. Why would I hurt you?" He stopped short, her last words seeming to suddenly hit home. Backing off a step, he studied her face a long moment, his mouth working into a line of silent surprise.

"You surely didn't think . . ." he began. "But you did! That's what's eating away at you! Mandy, I wasn't suggesting we share a room. What kind of jerk do you take me for anyway? Even if I had thought you might, don't you think I'd at least have asked? That was the furthest thing from my mind."

To see him following so plainly now the direction her misguided thoughts had taken, to see the look of surprise on his face reflecting a clean conscience was

110

more humiliation than she could bear. The tears she'd held by a slender thread slipped from between thick lashes and slid down flaming cheeks.

There was a gentleness in his sinewed strength as he gathered her close, a tenderness in his low admission, "Well, maybe not the furthest. But I wasn't going to take advantage of you, Mandy. Come on now. Quit with the tears."

He cradled her close, his musky-scented shirt absorbing her tears, his chin resting on the top of her head. "I'm really kind of hurt you'd think me such a conceited cad. I'll claim a little decency, even if the pull between us *is* strong, maybe even stronger than you realize. But . . ."

Mandy put a silencing hand on his mouth. She didn't want to hear him explore aloud what she considered to be the most private of thoughts, thoughts that meshed with hers in a most disconcerting way. Especially not when she was standing so close, their heartbeats seemed one, so close she breathed the clean masculine scent of him and felt the manly strength of his body next to her. Nerve endings all through her being were making their presence known in new and disturbing ways.

A slight tremor shook her as she swallowed her last sob and his arms tightened. It was a tight-rope she walked, a yawning killer of a gorge down below and she knew it very well, knew enough to put a little more distance between them too.

On the pretext of getting a tissue, she crossed the carpeted room. A shaky laugh broke the tension between them. "I'm as bad as Ellen," she claimed. "All these tears for nothing."

"Ellen's a rain-face too?" Gently teasing, he came to join her.

Mandy nodded. "Ellen's having a time of it, getting ready for her wedding. She broke down tonight and had quite a crying jag. I played doctor and told her if

111

she didn't get her mind off the wedding for a few hours, she was going to be a basket case.

"Physician, heal thyself, eh?" Mandy sniffed and wiped away her final tear.

"I wouldn't call yours a jag, exactly," he said lightly. "Just a brief summer shower, preceded by a lot of thunder and lightning. But maybe there's a rainbow in the making. Smile for me, Mandy, then we'll talk some more about the weekend."

Her heart knocked loudly in her chest. He still wanted her to go, despite how badly she'd thought of him.

She gave him the smile he'd requested, then allowed him to lead her to the sofa. Folding himself down beside her, T.K. released a lusty sigh.

"I guess maybe the solution to your discomfort about going away with me for a weekend would be to take someone with us."

"T.K., I misunderstood," Mandy said, hot with remorse. "Will you forgive me for thinking so low of you?"

To her surprise, he chuckled. "Let's face it, your trust quota is low, but your judgment might prove better than mine. Would you jump up and toss me out if I said you're pretty hard to resist?"

Mandy ducked her head to avoid his sharp gaze. His voice was like a beaded chain threaded with honesty, low-keyed amusement and yes, desire. Unsure which of the three she found the most disturbing, Mandy pleaded, "Let's not talk about it."

"Why not? It isn't going to go away. I say let's put it all out in the open and decide how to handle it."

Practicality came so easy to him! Writhing in embarrassment, Mandy objected, "That's so analytical."

Amused at the distaste in her voice, he slanted her a dry look. "Honestly Mandy, I don't know what to make of you. One minute, you're thinking with your head, the next with your heart. I'm just weak enough to follow any path your heart might take, but you'd hate me later, so let's be practical. Let's take someone with us. How about this sister of yours, Ellen? Would she be able to get away? And her fiancée too?''

Mandy exclaimed, ''That's a great idea! Ellen loves bright lights and excitement. It's just what she needs to get her mind off the wedding. I'll call her right now. That is, if you're sure you don't mind. I mean, not knowing Ellen or Gregory . . . it won't be awkward for you, will it?''

His finger-tips brushed a curl back from her temple, sending small shivers of pleasure through her. ''Only if they park themselves between us,'' he said.

Confused, but needing to reassure him, she said, ''They won't.''

His lips followed the path his fingers had taken. ''That's good,'' he said. ''Because if they did, I'd feel obligated to ditch the pair of them. And when I put my mind to it, I'm good at ditching.''

Almost a premonition it seemed, the dull ache in her throat at his flippant admission. Before his kisses could erase the caution draping her emotions, she moved away from him.

''I'd better call Ellen right away. This isn't much warning, and Gregory runs a tight schedule. Did I tell you he was a dentist?'' she rambled on, making her way to the phone, fighting the potent feelings his close proximity induced.

''Fascinating,'' he murmured, his eyes glinting knowingly. He stirred then from his position on the sofa and said he'd leave her to her ''arranging.''

''Call me and let me know the out-come,'' he added, as he let himself out the door.

Ellen was taken with the idea, though a bit miffed that Mandy had kept T.K. such a secret.

''And me, your only sister,'' she chided.

"Even if I'd told you, Ellen, you wouldn't have listened, unless the word 'wedding' or 'Gregory' was in the same sentence," Mandy defended herself.

Ellen admitted it with a giggle. "But you should have told me, anyway," she added. "Is he cute?"

A flutter took charge of Mandy's midriff as she considered T.K.'s drawing power. "He is very . . . male, I guess is the word. And if you weren't eight days from the altar, I'd have second thoughts about introducing you. I don't need any competition. Corey's already warned me he's quite a hit with the ladies."

"Corey? What's he got to do with it?"

"They happen to be partners at Four Seasons," Mandy informed her.

"What a weird triangle," Ellen muttered. "What does Corey think of you throwing him over for his partner?"

Mandy issued an exasperated sigh. "In the first place, I don't think he knows T.K. and I are dating. Even if he did, it wouldn't matter. Corey and I have never been more than friends."

"I'll believe *that* when Corey stops looking at you like he could gobble you whole. He's wild over you!" Ellen giggled again.

"Pooh. He has a list of girl friends thicker than the yellow pages."

"If you say so." Ellen stopped her teasing. She was in a rush to call Gregory and present him with the Branson idea. It wasn't long before she phoned back to say Gregory wanted to go, but that he had a full schedule of appointments on Friday and couldn't possibly make Branson before eight o'clock Friday evening.

Mandy phoned T.K. and plans were finalized. She and T.K. would leave for Branson early in the afternoon, thereby having time for some sight-seeing before dinner.

"I'll call ahead and have them hold four tickets at the ticket office for the Shepherd of the Hills play, then Ellen and Gregory can meet us there, all right?" T.K. ended.

"Fine," Mandy agreed. Reluctant though she was to end the conversation, she was remembering Miss Princeton's cat Willie with a guilty conscience.

However, upon crossing the hall, she learned that the Murphy girls had already found Willie and returned him home.

"I was on my way over to tell you, but you had a gentleman caller and I didn't wish to intrude," Miss Princeton added, eyes frankly curious. "I don't recall seeing him around here before."

On a light-hearted impulse, Mandy gave Miss Princeton a wide grin. "You probably haven't. He's new. Isn't he adorable?"

The elderly Miss Princeton tittered like a young girl. "Adorable isn't quite the word. I peeked out the door and from my vantage point, he appeared all male and, I might add, a little familiar."

"Perhaps you ran into him last Saturday when he brought me home," Mandy suggested, deliciously warmed by the mere mention of his name.

Miss Princeton wrinkled her forehead in thought. "No, I don't think so. His isn't a face I'd forget. It was more like being reminded of someone else. I know!" she exclaimed waving her hands about. "He reminded me a bit of your other gentleman friend. Much more commanding, of course, but something in the facial structure. They aren't by chance related?"

Mandy trickled laughter. "I hardly think so, Miss Princeton. They *are* business partners, though."

Thoughtfully, Miss Princeton remarked, "They say marriage partners come to favor one another after a time. Perhaps it's true of business partners too."

Amused by the idea, Mandy smiled and told her neighbor good-night. Far too excited to sleep, Mandy went to the sewing machine. Not until crisp lime-shaded linen fabric was transformed into a tailored skirt and vest for Claire Manson did she give in to her yawns and go to bed. Even then, it was some time before the churning anticipation within let her rest.

A glorious June sun was shooting through the curtains, heating her apartment by the time Mandy awoke the next morning. Letting a hunk of left over cornbread and an apple pass for a late breakfast, Mandy began packing her suitcase.

That task completed, she showered, styled her hair loose about her face and slipped into a white eyelet sundress, tying a blue satin ribbon at the waist for a touch of color.

After dabbing on a minimum of make-up, she frowned at the clock. Anticipation seemed to have slowed the passing of time. Several hours remained before T.K. would come. She made a brief call to Ellen to tell her they would leave the two tickets, for seats which adjoined theirs, at the box office so there wouldn't be a mix up in trying to make connections.

Too restless to be cooped up any longer, Mandy went to make delivery on Claire Manson's skirt and vest outfit. Her joyous heart spilled over as she hummed along to a love song playing on the radio. Two songs and a dozen stop-lights later, she slowed for Claire's horseshoe shaped driveway.

A familiar late-date Corvette sat in front of the house. A smile crept to her lips. No wonder Corey'd been making himself so scarce of late.

The middle-aged housekeeper Mandy knew only as "Neta" met her at the door. She smiled recognition.

"Claire'll be glad to see you. She's been fabric shopping again," Neta said, opening the door wide. "Come right in."

Neta clucked disapproval. "That woman! She's got enough clothes to outfit half of Stratton now. Every closet in this house is crammed full and she just keeps addin' to it, she does."

Having no wish to discuss her client's zeal for new clothes, Mandy said with a twinkle in her eye, "You won't hear me complaining."

"Pay good, does she?" Neta asked, not the least uncomfortable about it. "Same here. I always say there's good in everybody if you just look far enough. With Claire, it's her easy way with money. Generous, she is. But I guess she can afford to be, her husband leavin' her so well off."

Edging her way back out the door, Mandy murmured, "Tell Claire I should have the rest of her order completed by a week from today."

The sound of footsteps on the parquet floor warned of Claire's approach even before she spoke.

"Is that Mandy, Neta? Don't let her get away! I want to show her that new fabric," Claire called out. The shapely young widow advanced, blinking her lovely eyes into adjustment from the outdoor glare as she slung a sheer yellow swim-suit cover-up over a skimpy bikini.

"Mandy, you're just the person I want to see. Mmm! Lovely," she murmured appreciatively, taking the lime-green outfit from beneath the clear plastic bag. "You do such fine work, darling, and so prompt. Let me pay you for this, then I have another teeny-weeny project I want to discuss with you."

"Neta?" she continued, turning to the housekeeper without breaking long enough to allow Mandy a reply. "Hang this in my upstairs closet, would you dear? I have a piece of cloth to show you, Mandy. Why don't you keep Corey company while I get it? He's out by the pool.

"Oh," she added, tossing off a casual look that fooled Mandy not in the least, "and would you be a dear and take him a drink? Poor man claims he's parched."

Well aware Claire was alerting her to her new standing with Corey, Mandy agreed amicably enough

117

despite her opinion that if Claire really wanted him, she was going about it all wrong. Corey could play fast and loose, but deep down there seemed to be a little boy need in him to be jerked into line. She'd long realized that was why they'd remained friends. He knew where she stood and he never belittled her for it.

The parquet floor gave way to a carpeted, melon-colored kitchen which oozed magazine cover perfection. On the glass-topped table, there was a tray containing two iced drinks. Mandy took one and stepped out onto the shaded patio. The pool, crystal clear in the sunlight, was just beyond the patio. Corey was draped in a lounge chair beside it, his back to her.

Prompted by a pinch of mischief, Mandy slipped up on sandaled feet, reached over his shoulder and put the icy glass in his hand. Head tilted back, eyes closed behind shaded glasses, he eased out a languid sigh.

"Thanks doll. You're the hostess with the mostest." He reached back and gave her a lazy slap on the thigh.

Leaping back, Mandy let out an indignant, "Hey!"

His eyes flew open, a look of pure confusion washing over him as he bounded out of his chair. "Mandy! I'm sorry. I thought you were Claire!"

His apology spewed out with such sincerity, she broke into laughter. "It serves me right, sneaking up on you like that."

"What are you doing here, anyway?" he demanded.

She chuckled again, for he wore the mask of the proverbial cat caught at play. "I came to deliver an outfit I'd finished for Claire. I won't bother asking what *you're* doing here."

"Claire invited me for a swim." Managing to sound guilty and self-righteous at the same time, Corey pushed a hand through his hair and for once, seemed at a loss for further words.

Suddenly sorry she'd teased him, Mandy said, "So

you and Claire are getting to be good friends. That's nice. Basically, I think Claire's lonely. You'll be good for her. You're so outgoing and fun."

"It's nothing serious," he said quickly. "I mean, like you said, we're just friends." A silent plea that was somehow poignant, dashed the sunshine from his jaunty smile. "You don't mind, do you Mandy? It isn't like I haven't tried to call you. Don't you ever stay home anymore?"

"Yes, I stay home occasionally and no, I don't mind about Claire. In fact, I think if you gave it time, you and Claire could be more than just friends."

Before the words were out, Corey was shaking his head. "No way, Mand. I'm just killing time, waiting for you to start taking me seriously."

Dismayed at what she saw in his eyes, Mandy said, "I've done you an injustice, Corey. You're too fine a man to be wasting your time on a girl with an obstinate heart."

Determination glazing his eyes, he said tersely, "That sounds a lot like good-bye." When she didn't deny it, his hand clutched her upper arm in a grip that hurt. "Uh-uh, Mand. I won't let you . . ."

"Mandy Holt, stop flirting with my Corey or I'll find a new seamstress," Claire surprised them both. Laughter followed her words, but Mandy saw the steel in her eyes.

Compassion washed over her. Claire loved Corey without even getting beyond his surface charm. And Corey couldn't see the goodness in Claire, a goodness she kept hidden beneath a veneer of classy toughness.

Claire began unfolding the length of material she held in her arms and offering explanations of her intentions for the fabric. Only half listening, Mandy stole a glance at Corey. Moments ago, he'd seemed so relaxed. Now he appeared tense and miserable.

"If you could have it by Monday," Claire broke into her thoughts, "I'll toss in a bonus. I've a luncheon meeting and . . ."

"I'm sorry, but I can't by Monday," Mandy interrupted.

"I know it's short notice," Claire said coaxingly, "but it's a fairly simple garment, isn't it? Couldn't you stitch it up in a couple of hours?"

"I could Claire, if I was going to be home."

Corey's head jerked around. He swept her with a questioning glance. She ignored it, but Claire didn't. She cashed in, turning it to her advantage where Corey was concerned.

"I see. Heavy weekend?"

Mandy turned away without answering. "If you'll excuse me, I must be going."

Claire followed her to the kitchen door, pressing the fabric upon her. "Take it anyway, Mandy. Whenever you finish it, let me know."

Nodding her agreement, Mandy looked back at Corey. His skin seemed pinched and tightly drawn over the high slope of his cheekbones. It hurt her to see him like that. She veered off her usual safe policy of keeping her nose out of other people's business and said to Claire,

"Corey is a fine man, Claire, but he's curious. I used to think he loved all women, a hopeless philanderer. I'm not so sure anymore, but that the right kind of woman might be able to hold him. It's almost like he's searching for something special. Something he's had a life-time of missing. Maybe he doesn't even know what," she struggled to a close, unable to capture her thoughts in clear words.

A cynical expression slashed Claire's face. Arching a finely plucked eyebrow, she suggested haughtily, "Something he sees in you, perhaps?"

Mandy denied it with a shake of her head. "He might think it's me, but it isn't. I'd bore him to tears. Maybe it's something hidden in you, Claire."

Claire issued a harsh laugh. "No, not by a long shot. I may be a lot of things, but I'm no fool. I know

120

when a man is out for a good time, period. And I can accept that. It fills the hours.''

"It's too little, Claire. You deserve more. So does Corey.'' Mandy further overstepped the boundaries of the professional relationship she established with all her clients. ''Don't give him what he wants, Claire. Make him hold out for the real you.''

"Not the glittering imitation that caught his eye, huh?'' she challenged, her voice a blend of resentment and self-mockery. ''You're saying now that I have his attention, play hard to get?''

Softly, Mandy replied, ''Don't play anything. Open up and be you.''

Startled into dropping her facade of blatant sensuality, Claire's face became as vulnerable as a child's. Her chin trembled ever so slightly. ''I'm afraid I've forgotten how.''

There was no easy reply. Perhaps if she'd possessed the wisdom of Gram's years, or even her father's, she could have found something meaningful to say, something to witness her faith. As it was, she said nothing and Claire turned away with a defeated sigh.

CHAPTER 8

Taking his eyes off the road a moment, T.K. said, "We'll see a show while we're here. That is, if you like country music."

"Would I be a true Ozark girl if I didn't?" Mandy countered. Her heart swelled at the lazy grin he tossed her.

"I don't know that you'd be any less an Ozark girl if you preferred classical. Or that soft, easy listening stuff they pipe into doctors' offices and elevators."

"I like that too," Mandy admitted. "But country gospel is my favorite. When Charlie Pride sings *Amazing Grace,* I get goose-bumps."

Braking to let a car in the other lane turn in front of them, T.K. chuckled. "I can't promise you Charlie Pride. But I feel safe in saying any show we see will be good entertainment. Guaranteed to get you laughing. Shall we pick one out for tomorrow night? Or would you rather wait and let Ellen and Gregory have a little in-put?"

"Unless you have a preference, let's let them choose," Mandy decided, for she wanted Ellen to feel a part of the plans too.

"Fine by me." He slanted her a quick glance as the traffic began crawling forward again. "I could do with something cold to drink. How about you?"

"Me too." Meeting his questioning grey eyes, a familiar warmth ran through her veins. Already she was having a wonderful time. Just being by his side. Having him consider her, yet take charge of all the bothersome details. Like the traffic!

"Lemonade shake-ups?" she suggested.

"A favorite of yours?"

Mandy nodded and he eased out a nostalgic sigh.

"County fairs, hot dogs on sticks, and the Ferris wheel. That's what lemonade shake-ups bring to mind. I know just the place. But let's drop the suitcases off at the motel first. It isn't much further."

The motel T.K. had chosen was a moderately plush two-story affair. The desk clerk gave them keys for the two rooms, one on each level. Given the option, Mandy chose the upper level.

The room had a balcony overlooking the pool. Enthralled by the gay scattering of umbrella-shaded tables, deck chairs and sun-bathers, Mandy would have lingered against the wrought-iron railing, but that T.K. set her suitcase inside the motel room, then whisked her off for the promised drink.

Cooling their thirst on icy shake-ups, they wandered from gift shop to gift shop making a few small purchases but mostly just looking and enjoying one another's company. Drifting into a mood of companionable ease, time slipped away.

At T.K.'s suggestion, they returned to the motel and parted company long enough to shower and change for dinner and the outdoor Old Mill Theatre.

The wine-colored blouse Mandy chose was long-sleeved, but thin and cool against her skin. The ruffle shawl collar dipped to a modest V and tied with a bow. Mandy fastened a fine gold chain around the lightly tanned column of her throat and inserted gold post earrings in her ears. She threaded a gold cord belt through the narrow belt hoops of her off-white, side-button linen skirt.

A quick brushing of her hair brought out the red highlights. It drifted to her shoulders in full soft curls and framed her heart-shaped face. A natural blush of excitement colored her delicately sculptured cheeks and deepened the rich color of her eyes.

She sat on the bed a moment, curling her toes into the thick shag carpet, comforting the ache of weary soles. But time was short and sore feet a sorry excuse for dawdling. Ignoring a protesting high arch, she slipped into dressy high-heeled open weave slides, dabbed her favorite fragrance on wrists and temples, then went out onto the balcony to kill the remaining minutes.

The pool and deck area below had emptied. The water was an inviting placid blue. Dinner pangs must have drawn them all away, Mandy mused, leaning against the railing.

Realizing she'd forgotten to slip her comb back into her pocketbook, Mandy returned inside to do so, then came out to the railing again. In her absence, a man had come out and was standing, with his back to her, attention focused on the pool.

Mandy studied him with casual interest. From her vantage point, he appeared tall. A burgundy knit shirt was molded to the muscular span of broad shoulders and tucked into crisp-pleated white dress slacks which favorably emphasized a narrow waist and lean hips. One hand left his pocket and made a run through dark, pleasantly rumpled hair.

Recognizing the mannerism before the man, her heart gave a jerk. Feeling foolish, she wondered how she could have missed recognizing T.K. even for an instant. In a few short weeks he'd become so much a part of her, she should have sensed his presence blind-folded.

A smile curved her lips as he glanced at his watch. She reached into her pocketbook for a coin, then let it fly. It hit the pavement at his feet and rolled toward the pool. He retrieved it, then peered up at the balcony.

"Penny for your thoughts," she called down to him.

Taking careless aim, he flipped the coin back up to her, challenging, "Penny for *yours*."

Laughing, she did a graceful pirouette. "I was hoping we won't be mistaken for twins."

He grinned. "At least we don't clash."

"Ellen will swear we planned it." She rested her slim brown arms on the railing. "She'll be green with envy. Gregory has steadfastly refused to wear matching bowling shirts. He's a dentist you know, and very conservative."

"Is he going to make me floss my teeth?" he teased and flashed her an even white smile.

"What? And discourage decay? Decay is his business."

Jingling his keys in his pocket, T.K. ended the light-hearted exchange. "Come on down from there. I'm hungry and you're giving me a crick in my neck."

Heart turning like a pin-wheel, Mandy locked her room and met him out by the pool. The restaurant he'd chosen had the atmosphere vacationers could appreciate, whether they were attired in evening clothes, or shorts, T-shirts and tennis shoes. There was the low hum of pleasant voices, waitresses in black skirts and vests and a portly chef who stole a minute from the kitchen to have a word with his customers. The menu boasted of the best open-pit barbequed beef the south had to offer, and before the meal was finished, Mandy gave them her vote.

But in T.K.'s company, fish and chips would have been no less enjoyable, Mandy mused. Comfortably full and content, she slipped off her shoes and relaxed into the bucket seat of T.K.'s Mercedes as they drove a winding road through wooded hills to reach the Old Mill Theatre.

The last mile or so of the drive, the traffic was stop and go as cars poured into parking lots. Because he was attentive to traffic, Mandy made no attempt to distract T.K. with idle chit-chat.

Being close enough to touch pleased her, if she but had the courage. His strong brown hands tempted her, alternately curling around the steering wheel and resting on the gear shift between them.

This afternoon she'd known the strength and warmth of his hand holding hers, for as they'd browsed through shops, he'd reached for her hand time and again.

At long last he got his turn and they exited off the road, into the parking lot. "Is it a long walk?" she asked. "I don't see anything but cars for miles."

His profile, so masterful only seconds ago in unguarded repose softened as he noted her stockinged feet, one rubbing the other.

"It's a ways yet. But if your feet are rebelling, there are jeep-drawn trailers shuttling back and forth to the theatre. We can hitch a ride."

"Does it make me a bad tourist if I give in to the temptation?"

He chuckled as he pulled into a parking slot and killed the motor. "You couldn't be a bad anything. Come on, Cinderella. Get into your golden slippers and let's go before we miss the frog-jumping contest."

Her heart knocked as he brushed up a memory. "I have no Cinderella dreams," she'd boasted so short a time ago, and mockingly, he was reminding her.

Did he know, as he flagged down the trailer caravan and helped her on, that today had brimmed full and run over with dreamlike qualities?

Snug against him on a crowded seat, Mandy was thankful for the ride, thankful too he'd been sensitive to her swollen feet. Tomorrow she'd wear more sensible shoes.

Tomorrow! How swiftly the hours were passing! If she could but capture each precious moment and hug them all to herself, never, never to let go!

A short time later, they sat near the front of the tiered, outdoor theatre, shoulders brushing, voices low as they chuckled over the honest to goodness frog jumping contest in the stage area below. It seemed to Mandy a slice of heaven on earth. Life was good. God was good. So good! Her senses soared on golden wing as her heart opened wide and embraced the fullness of life.

Ellen and Gregory arrived at dusk, just moments before the show began. While Mandy made introductions, T.K. shook hands with Gregory and gave Ellen a slow friendly smile that surprised a jealous twinge in Mandy.

The failing light didn't hamper Ellen's eyesight. Her surprised gaze shuttled from T.K. to Mandy, over to Gregory and back to Mandy again.

"You didn't tell me he was so good-looking," she whispered in Mandy's ear, then launched into a breathless account meant for the ears of the men too.

"I was afraid we were going to be late. Gregory never fudges on the speed limit, do you honey?" She arched him a loving smile. "And we drove with the top down because it is such a gorgeous evening, so here we are, road dust and all."

Ellen's smile fanned them all, lingering curiously on T.K. "Why, you two match! Gregory look, will you? Isn't that sweet?"

"We didn't plan it," Mandy murmured for poor Gregory's sake, and caught T.K.'s grin out of the corner of her eye.

Ellen paid no attention. "I keep telling you honey, it isn't hokey to match. *Now* will you go along with the his and hers bowling shirts?"

Gregory said with dry humor, "Yes, and I'll wear mine inside out for that individualistic touch."

"You!" Ellen gave him a playful pinch on the shoulder. He retaliated by wrapping an arm around the back of her chair and whispering in her ear. Ellen giggled and devoted the remaining minutes until show time to behaving herself.

"Effervescent, isn't she?" T.K. whispered to Mandy.

"That's Ellen, all right," she whispered back. "When she's up, she's really up and when she's down, we all suffer. She drives Gram and Dad and I a little crazy sometimes, but we love her dearly."

"I can see that you do," came his low answer. "And it's apparent the feeling is mutual. You're lucky, Mandy."

The touch of sadness in his voice made her blurt, "Is it lonesome, not knowing your brother . . . rather, your half-brother?"

His eyes shifted away from her face to study the scenery below. "I *do* know him, and it's still lonesome," he murmured at long last.

Mandy held her surprise in check, wondering why she'd assumed that wasn't the case. Perhaps it was because the few times he'd mentioned his half-brother, his comments had been brief, as if their paths never crossed.

Was it the dusk that seemed to throw closed curtains over his features, or was he intentionally shutting doors on the subject? Either way, she wasn't about to ask questions. They'd come so far today, getting to know the little inconsequential things that went into forming a tight friendship. If this half-brother was a can of worms he wanted left sealed, then so be it.

Once the show began, Mandy was quickly drawn into the drama and action, though Ellen's whispering was a momentary distraction.

"He really *is* quite handsome."

Mandy looked at the bearded old-timer occupying center stage. "Who, him?"

Ellen giggled. "No, silly. T.K. Impressive is the word."

"What'd you think? I'd fallen for a fellow only a mother could think pretty?"

"No. But after Corey, you have to admit he's . . . Corey! Hey, does he know about T.K.?" Ellen changed the subject mid-stream. "I hope, I hope," she added under her breath.

Mandy looked at her sharply. "I haven't told him and I don't think T.K. has either. Why?"

Even in the dark, Ellen's wince was discernible. "He must have his nose to the wind, then. He came by the house this afternoon, looking for you. I tried to be vague Mandy, but you know how persistent he is. I finally told him where you'd gone just to shake him loose."

"And I suppose you told him who I was with, too?"

Ellen admitted it with a nod and asked when Mandy sighed, "Does it matter?"

"I suppose not. I've been postponing the inevitable. But it's a bit awkward, with he and T.K. being partners."

Before she could say anything further, T.K. slid an arm around her shoulder and turned her face toward the stage, saying, "You're about to miss something important here, and if you do, the rest of the story won't make much sense, unless of course, you've read the book."

She confessed that she hadn't.

"Then you and Ellen better stop whispering and listen," he suggested.

It wasn't hard, heeding his suggestion for the native actors poured heart and soul into their parts, sucking her into the story until once again, she was watching and listening with rapt attention.

Time passed, the thread of the tale evoking emotions ranging from poignancy over love lost to righteous anger over injustice and greed. By the time the echo of the last line faded, Mandy had blinked back her share of tears. She rose from her theatre seat glad of the throngs of people giving her time to immerge emotionally from the story into the reality of a soft, southern night.

"May as well take our time," T.K. murmured, a guiding hand on the small of her back. "Traffic is going to be murder getting out of here."

At the same time, Ellen was turning back to say, "Gregory and I are going to run, see if we can't beat the crowd. Are you with us?"

Mandy gave her shoes a rueful glance and shook her head. "Here, you take the room key." T.K. fished his key from his pocket too and turned it over to Gregory. As they disappeared into the blackness of the night, T.K. chuckled.

"I have a feeling Gregory is going to have his hands full with her."

Mandy agreed with a sentimental, "I hope he'll be kind."

They waited a while for a jeep-drawn trailer with room for two more. By the time they reached the parking lot, out-flowing traffic was a jam.

Eventually, they pulled onto the road, and talked away the miles back to town. Though it was late, Mandy had never felt more wide awake.

"Ready to turn in?" T.K. asked, as he helped her from the car, then paused to lock it.

"Not really. It's a beautiful night, isn't it?" Mandy turned her face up to the clear star-studded sky.

"Would you like to sit by the pool awhile?" he asked, and Mandy was quick to agree. T.K. seemed restless though, more inclined to wandering along the side of the pool than sitting in the deck chair beside her.

"I'd like to have a pool," he confided, "but Mrs. Hart frowns on the idea. She thinks it would detract from the dignity of her precious colonial mansion."

He said it without rancor, and Mandy found his consideration for Mrs. Hart's opinions a touching contradiction to his male dominance.

"It *is* your house," she murmured. "I don't suppose Mrs. Hart would quit if you did go against her wishes and have one installed."

"No, but it's awkward. She has her heart set on preserving the place, keeping it as it was a hundred years ago and I have to admit, there's value to the history of it.

"But it's like living in a museum. I do enough promotional traveling, it doesn't get to me too much. But Grand-dad says he feels enough of a museum piece himself without living like one."

He chuckled softly and a small silence ran between them as he paced the length of the pool. "Did you see the sign?" he called back to her. " 'No life-guard on duty. Swim at your own risk.' "

Reminded of their first meeting at Danny's Market, Mandy joined him murmuring, "You're a great one for reading signs, aren't you?"

His voice laced with a challenge, he asked, "Shall we take the risk?"

"Swim? At this time of night? You're kidding!"

"Not at all. We'd have the pool all to ourselves. What do you say?" he asked, persuasion in his every cadence.

He took advantage of her silence. Giving her a little push, he ordered, "Go change into your suit. I'll meet you back here in five minutes."

It was more like ten, thanks to Ellen. She played twenty questions while Mandy changed into a multi-striped bandeau suit and a short yellow terrycloth cover-up.

"Where are you going now? And you say *I'm*

131

impulsive! I still can't get over how good looking he is. Are you sure he's safe? Mandy, stand still a minute. Look at me! Just as I thought. You're positively starry-eyed! It's a good thing I came along to keep an eye on you."

Ignoring Mandy's blustery protest, Ellen flung herself down on the bed and released a delicious sigh of contentment. "I'm having a terrific time. I feel more relaxed than I have in months and I haven't mentioned the you-know-what even once." Suddenly, she pursed her lips. "A midnight swim. Maybe I ought to go with you."

Mandy edged toward the door. "You and Gregory could come."

Regretfully, Ellen shook her head. "Gregory's probably already in bed. Say, how about bringing me back a soft drink?"

"You'll still be up?"

Ellen bobbed her head and came off the bed to push a towel into Mandy's hands. "I'm not going to bed until I've heard all about this romance of yours. And don't forget the soft drink!" she called as Mandy walked out.

T.K. was in the pool, parting the water with sure, strong strokes, hardly causing more than a ripple. Mandy dropped her wrap and towel on a chair and went to test the water with her foot. It felt comfortably cool. She sat on the fiberglass edge and dangled her legs. The surface water still retained some of the heat of the sun, while down deeper, it was more brisk.

T.K. joined her at the edge. "That's no way to get used to it. You have to take the plunge."

"I'll do it myself, thank you." Mandy skittered back as he tugged at one foot. Laughing, he let go, then dove under to reappear at the far end of the pool. Mandy went to the steps and tried easing in that way. It wasn't any easier. He was right, of course. One quick plunge was the surest way to adjust to the temperature. She lingered on the top step, the water lapping her ankles.

T.K. swam to her and stood a moment in water waist high, watching her. "Ready to race?" he asked, and climbed the three fiberglass steps.

It hardly seemed a fair match, she thought, for his upper body was taut and muscular, as were his legs. Mistrusting the mischief dancing in his eyes, she backed off saying, "I have to get used to the water first, then I'll race."

"To get used to it, you have to get in," he pointed out, closing the distance between them. Droplets of water glistened upon his dark hair and face.

The clean male scent of him teased her senses as his hands curled around the soft flesh of her upper arms and he pulled her to him. Her heart whirled like a windmill and a rush of sound filled her ears, blotting out the passing traffic, the settling in of weary vacationers, the chirrup of a lone cricket keeping watch in some hidden crack.

"T.K.," she murmured his name on a caught breath as he muzzled the delicate line of her jaw from chin to earlobe.

"Hmm?"

Hesitant lips formed the words, "Maybe we should go in."

His mouth touched her temple. "Not until we've raced."

The only thing racing was her heart. She tried desperately to steady it as his lips traveled a downward path to claim hers. They taunted and tantalized until she stopped trying to hold herself aloof.

The tough harshness of his arms holding her close ignited a passion that threatened to burn out of control. Her hands stole around his neck, relishing the damp coarseness of his hair, then linking together to hold on, to pull closer, to draw the moment out. His kisses seared her very soul and she clung to him in

133

awed reverence, knowing she could never belong to another. It was T.K. or no one, her fate was sealed.

He whispered her name on a shaky breath of regret, then broke the embrace to scoop her into his arms and unceremoniously toss her into the pool.

"T.K.!" his name ripped from her throat in a squeal as her body was plunged from fire into ice.

"Swim or sink!" he ordered gruffly and dove over her head.

Swallowing a mouthful of chlorine water, coughing and sputtering, she clung to the side of the pool and thought, how right he is! His promise to control the feelings came crashing to mind.

Thank the Lord someone was in control! The water cooled her blush of despair. She kicked off from the side and began swimming, one stroke after another, passing T.K. without speaking or touching, burning off energy with lap after lap until her lungs ached and her arms and legs went weak.

When she felt she could not swim another stroke, she climbed onto the top step and gulped air into her punished lungs. T.K. kept swimming, back and forth, back and forth, like a fish trapped in a bowl too small to contain him.

Shivering, Mandy went for her wrap, then dropped down on the step again with only her feet in the water. T.K. climbed out at the other end, draped a towel across his shoulders and came to sit beside her. An empty silence hung between them.

She could hear the cricket again, sawing his legs together. An occasional car passed on the street and somewhere in the motel, a balcony door closed.

T.K. gave his hair a brisk towel drying. "Mad?"

"No." She searched his face in the darkness, making out planes and angles, but not his expression. "Should I be?"

He shrugged his broad shoulders. "Last time I kissed you like that you got in a huff and took yourself

134

out of my life," he said in that frank way she found so disconcerting.

She stirred from her silence. "That was due to a misunderstanding. We straightened it out."

"Because we *talked* it out. If we hadn't, you wouldn't be here right now."

"And that would matter to you?" she couldn't help asking.

"Yes, it would matter. That's why I'm asking, before any misunderstandings can crop up."

She shook her head. "No, T.K. I'm not mad. You made a promise and you kept it." No thanks to me, she thought, her face growing warm.

"Don't put too much stock in that," his voice took on a note of gravel. "I'm flesh and blood too."

And she'd tried him to the limit? Was that what he was saying? In a small voice, she said, "I'm sorry."

"I'm not!" There was a depth of feeling to his words that brought fresh waves of heat to her face. From now on, she vowed, midnight swims were out. Even now, he had only to hold her in his arms again and she'd go spiraling into a repeat flight of madness.

"Let's change the subject," she suggested, and turned her head to make out his quick, knowing grin.

"All right. Let's talk about this." With a cool finger, he traced the scar on her leg.

It was a scar that seemed so much a part of her, she forgot it was there most of the time. Maybe that was because remembering brought pain.

"That is where I got my phobia for dogs."

"You mentioned you'd been bitten. Want to tell me about it?"

It surprised her to find that she did. Somehow it was important that he understand her feelings. She launched into the account of the stray dog which had wandered to their house when she was a small child.

It had been a few days after her father had taken her aside and told her with tears in his voice that her

135

mother wasn't going to be with them much longer, that God was taking her home. She'd known her mother had been suffering in the last weeks and months, yet she hadn't wanted to lose her. She'd been so scared and lonely. Gram had been there too, nursing her mother and taking care of Ellen, who was a very lively four-year-old at the time.

Gram, she recalled, had taken a dislike to the dog on sight. Her father hadn't liked him either, but he'd given into Mandy's pleadings and let her keep it.

That dog had seemed to her a safe harbor in a storm tossed world. She cared for him, and talked to him constantly, confiding all her worst fears. Yet because she'd been so young, she hadn't seen that the dog remained totally aloof.

Then came the day he'd gotten into the pigs and killed a piglet. Her horror had given way to the certainty her father would have the dog put down. Intentions purely protective, she'd wanted to hide the dead baby pig before her father came home. But when she'd come between the dog and his kill, he'd turned on her.

Mandy trailed her fingers in the water as she came to the worst part of the story. "Mother heard my screams. She hadn't been any further than a chair by the window in weeks, so I guess it was God-given strength that enabled her to get to me at all. By that time, the dog had run off with the piglet. Mother carried me into the house, then collapsed."

Even after all the years of healing, it was hard to remember without experiencing the anguish all over again. Mandy blinked hard on threatening tears and finished.

"Gram took us both to the hospital. I came home with twenty-one stitches in my leg. Mother didn't come home at all."

She looked at him then, wondering if he could understand how hard it was for a young child to feel guilty and angry and empty all at the same time.

136

"And you blamed the dog?" he prompted, turning her face up to the star-light.

"Yes. And you know, I think I felt a little cheated when I came home from the hospital and found Dad had already had the dog destroyed. I wanted someone to hang all that hurt on."

"So if not *the* dog, any dog would do?"

Gently spoken though they were, Mandy was stung by his words. "I was six years old, T.K."

"But you're all grown up now."

"I never said my fear was logical," she countered defensively.

With one hand he lifted her damp hair off her shoulders. His lips touched the sensitive nape of her neck. "I'm not criticizing," he said. "Just wishing you didn't have to be afraid any longer. Next to Grand-dad and you, dogs are what I like best."

His voice cajoling, he coaxed a little smile from Mandy. "It isn't that I *want* to be afraid," she murmured, his lips playing havoc with her heart.

"Then maybe there is hope we can give you the cure. How about driving out some evening next week and taking a look at the pups? We have a litter four weeks old and one six weeks, just ready for new homes. You wouldn't be afraid to hold one, would you? They're irresistible, take my word."

Thinking it was *him*, not puppies, she found irresistible, Mandy said, "I might give it a try."

"Good girl." He gave her a hug, and she wrapped her arms around his neck and got a kiss out of the bargain too.

"Your sentinel up on the watch tower is getting restless," he said, an edge of humor marking his voice as he disengaged her arms from around him. "That *is* the balcony off your room isn't it?"

Mandy looked up and made out the shadow too. Knowing a pang of remorse, she said, "It's Ellen. I promised to bring her a cold drink after our swim."

"She's not doing body-guard duty?"

Features warming, Mandy said, "I think she would have liked to swim really, but Gregory had already turned in. Or so she thought."

"He had," T.K. confirmed. "But she could have come with you anyway."

"She was afraid she'd be a tag-along," Mandy said.

"She would have been." He grinned and gave her one last kiss. "But why don't you call her down anyway, and we'll all go to the coffee shop together. I'm sure it's open all night."

Thinking it very sweet of him to include Ellen, Mandy went to get her while T.K. donned a T-shirt and sweat-pants over his swimming trunks.

Much later, Mandy called sleepy replies across the darkened room as Ellen delved into her relationship with T.K. If Mandy hadn't been so joyously happy, she would not have been so readily lead into sharing her feelings.

"Have you known him long?" Ellen asked.

"A few weeks."

"But you've gone out a lot in those few weeks?" Ellen was uncustomarily persistent.

"No," Mandy admitted. "Most of the time, we've spent misunderstanding one another. But I think we're getting the hang of communication finally."

"I think you are too. That is, judging from what was going on down there by the pool," came her sister's dry comment.

"That's tacky, Ellen. I wouldn't spy on you and Gregory." Mandy punched her pillow into shape.

"Then your sisterly concern must be pretty low on the meter!" Ellen exclaimed. "I was just about to put on my swimsuit and come down, when he tossed you in the pool. Just in time, too. The pair of you needed a cooling down."

"Ellen! Don't you lecture me. I'm the big sister here, remember?" Mandy said defensively.

"Yes, but I'm the one who has been tested by fire and I could give you a pointer or two, if you'd but ask."

"Such as?"

"Take it a little slower. It seems to me you hardly know him. You admit yourself it has been a short time."

"But quality time. I wouldn't trade the time we've spent together for anything. I feel I know him, Ellen," she said. "I feel I can trust him."

"You'd better can the feelings and use your head."

A bit surprised by the serious turn the conversation had taken, Mandy propped herself up on one elbow and asked, "You and Gregory never get carried away?"

"Getting carried away is easy," Ellen said. "It's surfacing before it's too late that's hard. Believe me, I know. The closer it gets to our wedding day, the harder it becomes. Especially when society makes it so acceptable to forget that God designed the intimacies between a man and a woman to be within the bonds of marriage. Something to strengthen the marriage."

Mandy leaned back into her pillow again, a little awed by Ellen. She had bubbled like a feather-head over all the trappings of her wedding and never in all the months of planning let on there were deeper concerns in her mind. The words she had spoken were in Mandy's heart too, but it helped to hear them aloud. For Ellen was right. It was easy to forget when the man you loved held you in his arms and made reason fade.

Hearing the covers in the next bed stir, Mandy turned her head to see the dim shadow of Ellen standing by her bed. "I wish you'd say something," she murmured. "Have I offended you, lecturing like Gram?"

Mandy scooted over and made room for Ellen.

139

"No, you haven't. Maybe you said some things I needed to hear."

The bed shifted as Ellen sat down and patted her hand. "God put the desire there, Mand. It's deep and natural and wonderful. Just as long as we remember not to cheapen the beauty of it by thinking we can have the pleasure without the commitment God intended."

"So what do you do, Ellen?" she asked in a small voice. "To keep from getting carried away, I mean?"

There was a smile in Ellen's reply. "It's more a matter of what I *don't* do. I don't go for midnight swims with the sky's brightest stars dim compared to the stars in my eyes. When the feelings are running strong, I steer Gregory toward the nearest crowd. Even if it's a crowd of only one. There's safety in numbers."

She giggled, sounding more like the light-hearted Ellen Mandy expected. "And," she finished, "I'm suggesting you do the same. I'd hate to have to cream that guy for breaking your heart. So take my two-cents worth and use it wisely."

Mandy murmured sleepily, "I'll give you your fee in the morning."

Ellen returned to her own bed and Mandy burrowed under the cool sheet, prayerfully considering all that Ellen had said. It wasn't too flattering, Ellen's obvious mistrust of T.K.'s intentions. But then, she had to admit as much as she loved T.K., there was no reason to believe her love was returned. He was attracted to her, attentive and unsecretive about the yearnings he felt, but that wasn't love.

It was pointless to stew. God, in His infinite wisdom knew the course before her and the outcome too. She would lean on him to keep the relationship pure and clean.

It was hard to say where her thoughts left off and prayer began. Prayer had long been that way with her, as natural as breathing and comforting as hugging a close friend. As she listened to the even sound of Ellen's sleep, her heart was full with gratitude for all the love in her life. Dad and Gram, Ellen, T.K. Even Corey crept into her thoughts and she whispered a prayer that things might be right between him and Claire, that they would not hurt or misuse one another.

As busy thoughts slowed, leaving her as calm and placid as the pool below her balcony, a new concern surfaced, catching her by surprise. It was a strong desire to no longer be burdened with her fear of one of God's creatures. Dogs were such an important part of T.K.'s life. She wanted to be an important part of his life too and how, Dear Lord, could that be when she could not deal with her fear?

"Lay it on the altar," Gram was fond of saying. That was what she did with her fear, humbly and prayerfully. Now if only God would pick it up and carry it for her!

CHAPTER 9

IT WAS A CAREFREE foursome who spent the next day roaming Silver Dollar City, the crafts capital of the nation. There was so much to see, it was hard to take it all in. But Ellen, towing Gregory along in the lead, tried.

The legendary tourist attraction had something to offer for everyone, be they connoisseurs of handicrafts modern and old, history buffs, or just out for good food and old-fashioned fun.

They tried out the rides before indulging in savory southern cooking. They clapped to the rhythm of Dixieland Jazz and cooled their thirst at the Silver Dollar Saloon just as Carrie Nation marched in to do her stuff. They cheered and hissed along with the crowd when the rainmaker gave a grand exhibition of his marvelous rainmaking machine. And they browsed in gift shops specializing in everything from blown-glass trinkets to woodcarvings to yester-years dolls.

It was early evening when weary feet were finally shown mercy, and after a quiet ride back to town, everyone was content to relax by the pool.

The pavement surrounding the pool still held the sun's warmth. Mandy lay with her eyes closed, smiling a little and making sleepy replies to Ellen's tireless chatter.

"Hope Gram likes the wind chimes. And Dad's sure to adore the book of poetry, don't you think, Mandy?"

Mandy managed a yawning response.

"That was sweet of you to remember Miss Princeton," she ran on. "The stuffed patchwork cat does look like her Willie."

"Only not so fat," Mandy murmured.

"Who was the candle for?" Ellen asked.

Mandy was reluctant to say she'd bought it for Corey. "It's just a gag gift."

"Did you see it?" Ellen turned to Gregory. "It has a wick at both ends."

Mandy flung an arm over her eyes, trying to drift back to the peaceful state nearing sleep.

Gregory hooked his towel around Ellen's slender throat. "How would you like for me to drag her off to the coffee shop and give you some peace, Mandy? What would it be worth?"

"A dollar. Put it on my tab," Mandy said.

"Her credit is terrible. She owes me two cents from last night," Ellen warned.

Mandy opened her eyes and grinned acknowledgment. In so doing, she startled an envious expression upon T.K.'s face. Too sleepy to put her finger on the cause, she closed her eyes again, and true to his word, Gregory hauled Ellen off to the coffee shop.

T.K. tickled her nose with the fringe of his towel. She tried to brush it away and he caught her hand. Turning it palm up, he delivered a leisurely kiss. A pleasant sensation stole up her arm as he moved closer.

"Who do you know burns the candle at both ends?" he asked.

"Hmm? Oh that. Like I told Ellen, it's a gag gift for a workaholic friend of mine."

"Do I detect an evasive note here?"

Mandy opened one eye, testing his interest. It seemed casual enough. She risked the truth. "It's for Corey."

He arched one dark brow. "Corey. Now there's a subject I'd like to pursue when you aren't so sleepy-headed."

She opened the other eye. It was inevitable they'd have to discuss him sometime. Why put it off? "Pursue away," she invited.

The prickly hairs on his leg brushed against her briefly as he shifted position. "I'm curious to know how you met him, if that isn't overstepping any boundaries of privacy. It's just that I wouldn't expect you to be lurking about any of Corey's regular hang-outs."

Did she detect a cutting edge to his voice? She propped up on one elbow, a position less vulnerable to attack, it seemed. "I met him at Pet World. He was trying to sell the manager on Four Seasons line of pet products when I happened along, buying something or the other for Miss Princeton's cat."

"That sounds like him," T.K. said abruptly. "Promoting sales is supposed to be my area of expertise."

Curiosity put words in her mouth. "You and Corey don't mix very well, do you?"

"Let's just say we can avoid clashing if we give each other plenty of space. And we do great by phone." His mouth twisted with cynicism.

"Isn't that awkward, doing business as partners when you aren't on friendly terms?"

"We try to be professional about it and not let personal feelings interfere. Most of the time it works out all right." His grey eyes lingered on her.

Aware she was on sticky ground and inviting a rebuke, she asked, "Why can't you be friends? What has happened?"

T.K. sat up straight and linked his arms around his knees. "Nothing happened," he said abruptly. "We've never been friends."

"I didn't get that impression from Corey."

His gaze, razor sharp, slashed back to her. "You've discussed me with Corey?"

"No." The admission tumbled out quickly, to ward off any misconceptions he might be forming. "He's always been very close-mouthed about you. He did say a long time ago, before you and I had met, that he'd met you in the army and the business involvement had grown from that. So I gathered you had been friends at one time."

T.K.'s laugh was short and cold. "Army buddies, huh. Well, he doesn't lack imagination."

Puzzled by this harshness in him, and yes, disappointed too, Mandy said, "Corey has a lot of fine qualities. He's ambitious, sure, but he's hard working. And he's really very likable. Most everyone likes him."

Sounding more curious than jealous, he said, "It's plain that *you* do."

"I do," she admitted freely. "Oh, he's strutty and macho sometimes, but behind it all, he's like a little boy wanting very much to be approved."

T.K. disagreed with a shake of his head. "You're wrong there. He could care less if I approve of him. Sometimes I think he goes out of his way to make sure I don't."

Mandy suggested, "Maybe he finds you a bit formidable, T.K."

"Me? Formidable? That's a laugh."

"Seriously. You have a pretty tough front. If you could see your face right now, you'd have to agree I'm telling the truth. It's closed up like a brick wall." She came up off her elbow and touched the shallow grooves framing his mouth.

His face softened. "Yeah, plain to see I'm scaring you to death."

145

"I wish it were different between you and Corey," she said, knowing she was treading shards of glass. "It isn't Christian of you, T.K."

"It isn't Christian of him either," he said harshly, though he didn't pull away from her fingers which crept up to explore the scar slashing his left eyebrow.

"Corey *isn't* a Christian. You can't expect him to behave as if he were. Whatever the hatchet is, why don't you bury it. Even if it means swallowing a dose of pride or making a sacrifice, wouldn't it be worth it?"

He did pull away then, muttering, "I could write a book on that."

"Then you have tried to mend the differences?" She used up her last ounce of courage in asking.

His head swung sharply around. "Who appointed you ambassador of peace, anyway? I'm beginning to wonder how deep this concern of yours goes for Corey."

Feeling as if she'd been slapped, Mandy caught her lip between straight white teeth and watched him dive into the water. How vulnerable love made her! She was close to tears, resenting his harsh treatment, yet simultaneously mesmerized by his lean, muscular body gliding through the water, powered by strong arm strokes.

Why had she pressed him? Was Corey important enough to allow a rift in her relationship with T.K.? Why *had* she pried and sermonized? It wasn't like her at all!

Because it was fast approaching the dinner hour and only a few faithful remained by the pool catching the sun's last rays, Mandy was left to wallow alone in her hurt, waiting, willing him to come back to her.

When he finally came, the strain between them was as painful as the distance had been. He stood rubbing dry the dark hair that matted his chest and looking as if he wished he could think of something to say.

146

"Getting hungry?" he asked finally.

Mandy shook her head.

"Well, I am. Let's get dressed and find a good restaurant." He turned away then, as if the choice was hers either to follow or to stay behind. He'd gone a good ten feet before he realized she'd held her place.

Turning, he asked in a clipped tone, "Aren't you coming?"

"Ellen has the door key."

He lingered a moment. "I guess you'll have to wait for her," he said finally and widened the distance some more.

Suddenly frightened and ready to have her pride slashed to ribbons if that was what it would take to reestablish harmony, Mandy came to her feet and called out to him.

"I'm sorry, T.K. It wasn't my place to question you. Don't leave me standing here."

He swore under his breath, she was sure that he did. But he came back to her growling, "Stop looking at me like that."

"I can't help it. I can't stand contention." The words in her throat felt as abrasive as the concrete beneath her bare toes.

"I don't know why it should bother you," he said. "Corey and I manage to live with it."

"I didn't mean you and Corey. I meant us."

Surprise stole the harsh lines from his features, and a moment later, she was in his arms, his heart-beat strong against her ear. The hurt drained away, leaving her awash with a love so intense she dared not think what sorrow it would be to lose him for good.

His words a soft whisper against her ear, he said, "Someday babe, when I don't feel so threatened by him, I'll explain about Corey. Okay?"

She didn't question his word "threatened," just lifted her head to ask, "You forgive me, then?"

He took one hand from the small of her back and

147

smoothed a tendril of hair back from her face. "There's nothing to forgive."

His lips had no more than brushed hers when Ellen came panting toward them, ordering, "Hey you two, break it up. Every restaurant in town is going to be filled if we don't get a move on."

Stepping away from him, Mandy said softly, "She has my best interests at heart."

"Darn her anyway," he tacked on, then added more seriously, "You're lucky, Mandy. You have a family who really cares about one another."

Her heart hurt for the wistful note in his voice. Didn't *his* family care? Kyle certainly did. His parents, dead now, surely had cared. His half-brother? Maybe she'd never know.

She gave him a parting kiss, then followed Ellen to dress for dinner and the country music show they planned to attend afterwards.

On Sunday morning, Gregory and Ellen accompanied T.K. and Mandy to services at a small country church. The members of the congregation offered the hand of Christian fellowship in a natural friendly way which put all four at ease.

T.K.'s strong bass mingled with Mandy's alto. Their hands touched as they held the hymnal and a thrill of sharing something very precious warmed Mandy to a toasty glow. The feeling lingered as they settled into their seats for the sermon.

Down-home country sense lined every crease of the minister's leathery face. He spoke simple words on his subject—a burden for the unsaved. Sincerity was mirrored upon his countenance as he shared Scriptures indicating God's people were to witness their faith in word and deed.

Witnessing. The very word made Mandy squirm on the inside. Wasn't it enough to serve in quiet ways?

As if reading her thoughts, the minister said in

closing, " 'Let your light shine before men in such a way that they may see your good works and glorify your Father who is in heaven.' "

"Those, my friends, are Jesus' words. I ask you. Does your friend, your neighbor, your fellow worker know the source of your Light? If not, won't you tell him soon that Jesus might be his Light and Salvation too?"

Moments later, Mandy moved with the flow of people toward the door. T.K.'s guiding hand was on her elbow, but Corey was on her conscience. The minister's words had hit home. Had she ever tried to lead Corey to God?

In front of her a man walking with a limp stopped to shake the minister's hand. "Should of worn my combat boots, preacher," she heard him say. "You gave my toes a good tromping."

"I stepped on my own toes too," the minister said. "Appreciate your coming this morning. I know these pews are hard on your back, acting up the way it has been. Don't worry about that hay field of yours. A couple of the boys and I will be out tomorrow and take care of it."

Impressed that the minister was a man of good acts as well as words, Mandy shook his hand and in response to his question, gave him her name.

"Have a safe trip home, and come worship with us again some time," he said warmly, reaching for T.K.'s hand.

"I appreciated your message," T.K. said.

"Then give God the glory. The words were His. I was only the instrument for proclaiming them," he replied.

His words lingered in Mandy's mind as they drove back to town. Was she guilty of not letting God use her as His instrument? Did she hoard the good news of God's plan of redemption under the guise of not wanting to push or force feed religion?

"You're awfully quiet," T.K. commented.

She surfaced from her preoccupation. "Ellen's talking enough for both of us."

Ellen, who was riding in the front seat with Gregory, turned and made a face at Mandy. "Don't pick on me or I'll start talking about the you-know-what!"

"What?" T.K. picked up on her threat. "What's she *not* talking about?"

"The wedding," Mandy told him. "She promised not to mention it all weekend."

"But the weekend is nearly over." Ellen sighed, for she and Gregory planned to start home after lunch. "I've had a super time. And I'm feeling relaxed and ready to face next weekend."

Gregory took his attention off traffic long enough to feign deep hurt. "Is marrying me that much of a strain on you?"

Giggling, Ellen scooted next to him and passed the remaining miles back to town assuring him whatever the strain, he was well worth it.

T.K. slid Mandy a grin. "Ain't love grand? Soothes the savage beast in Gregory, sure enough," he murmured for her ears alone.

His smoky grey eyes so warmly intent upon her face ignited fireworks in her heart, and for a while she put Corey and the morning's sermon in cold storage.

Because the noon meal was to be their last in Branson, Ellen and Gregory drew it out, lingering over coffee and keeping up an easy flow of conversation. But the time came when they returned to the motel, packed their belongings and turned in the room keys.

Though Gregory and Ellen started for home, T.K. turned his car toward the lake road, saying with a wicked grin, "Would you trust me to take you out on the lake for a row with your body guard gone?"

"A row?"

Lines of amusement fanned out from his eyes. "I'd squire you around in something speedier, but my boat hasn't been checked out yet this summer."

"A row boat is fine," Mandy assured him. Rather romantic, actually, she thought to herself, admiring a sudden flurry of elegant homes built along the shore-line of Lake Taneycomo.

The lake itself skipped in and out of view as T.K. traveled the winding road with the familiarity of one who knew what lay around the next bend. It occurred to Mandy she'd been very obtuse all weekend.

"You must vacation here every summer!"

He nodded. "My parents kept a house on the lake front, and I've never gotten around to disposing of it. So I make use of it occasionally."

The house soon came into view, an attractive A-frame structure nestled in a small grove of trees with the lake lapping at the sloping backyard.

T.K. took life jackets from a garage which held in storage a variety of water-sporting equipment, then lead the way to the dock. There was a small weather-beaten rowboat nearly hidden by the uncut grass. T.K. tossed the life jackets into the bottom of the boat and manipulated it around until it hugged the dock. After he'd put the oars in place, he held out a hand to Mandy.

"Hope she hasn't sprung any leaks over the past year."

Affecting an equal calm, Mandy asked, "Should we take along a bucket for bailing her out?"

"No." He grinned and promised, "I'll keep us within swimming distance of shore.

"You'd better keep us within walking distance of it," Mandy retorted. She took her seat in the stern of the boat and settled the skirt of her dainty-print sundress around her. "I don't like getting doused unless I'm dressed for it."

T.K. sat facing her, the muscles in his sun-browned

arms rippling as he handled the oars with a smooth grace that made the chore appear effortless.

Not to be lulled into listlessness by the lazy, lapping sound of the water caressing the boat, Mandy said, "Let me row. It looks like fun."

"You know how?"

"No. But how hard can it be?" she said, ready to change places with him.

"By all means, be my guest." There were lights of laughter in his eyes as with a sweeping bow, he gave her his place. It didn't take the laughter long to erupt from his lips, along with half a dozen instructions.

"The other way, Mandy. Move the water the other way, we're going backwards. That's better. No, straighten her out. Pull with the left oar, just the left."

Beads of perspiration dotted her brow and her arms began to ache. The boat under her direction went backward, sideways and in circles. "Just a second, I'll get the hang of it soon," she objected when T.K. tried to resume the chore. "Let me do it."

"I can't. Boating in circles is kind of like kissing you. It makes me dizzy," he teased, the laughter in his eyes giving way to tenderness. "Which isn't a bad idea," he added.

"Sit down! You're rocking the boat!" Mandy's voice rose in alarm as he joined her on the seat.

"You've been rocking my boat ever since we met," he accused, his voice smooth as velvet against her ear.

He put the oars out of harms way and slipped his arms around her. His lips, light as butterfly wings, caressed her hair-line, then took a downward path to possess her lips.

Gentle though they were, his kisses nearly stole the words, "I love you" from her lips. He lifted his mouth from hers and she nestled against him, savoring the male scent of after-shave lotion and thinking wistfully if only her love was returned!

His lips brushed the top of her hair, then he loosed his hold and looked back in the direction of the A-frame house. A dry chuckle left his throat.

"Ellen's given me a complex. I feel like we're being watched."

Mesmerized by his closeness, Mandy said, "Ellen's halfway home by now," and lifted her face to welcome his lips again.

"I didn't bring you out here for this," he said, pushing her away from him. "There's something I feel I must tell you. And I don't quite know how to start."

His fine grey eyes reflected his hesitancy and Mandy's heart lurched with misgivings. He blew out a sigh and motioned toward the seat in the stern of the boat.

"Why don't you give me a little distance, before I change my mind and my intentions?"

Reacting to his brusque tone, Mandy did as he requested, but she felt suddenly bereft, as if the distance separating them could not be measured in a few mere feet. What was it he was so near to confessing that lined his brow with such somber intensity?

"We came very near to quarrelling over Corey yesterday," he began, his white-knuckled grip on the seat belying his calm tone.

Mandy shifted uncomfortably. "I spoke out of turn. It isn't for me to say what sort of relationship you should have with Corey. He's your partner, not mine."

"Corey is more than my partner. He's my brother." T.K.'s voice was deadly quiet, but unmistakably clear.

A small tremor of shock went through her. "Your brother?"

Face grim, a haunting sadness lurking in his eyes, T.K. nodded. "I mentioned my mother had a child by a previous marriage? That child was Corey."

153

Mandy was reeling with the unexpectedness of his revelation. "But why the big secret? I've known Corey for over a year and he's always given me the impression he had no family. Living, anyway," she qualified.

Bitterness crept into his response. "That's because he gets some kind of perverted pleasure out of disowning our relationship. I don't know. Maybe he thinks we let him down when he needed us, so he's retaliating in the only way he can.

"Only a handful of people know we're brothers. And they are the old-timers who remember my mother's brief marriage to Corey's father. It ended, as you may have guessed, in a very nasty divorce. I guess maybe Corey bears a few scars over it."

Baffled that two brothers who'd grown so far apart would form a business partnership, Mandy discarded several half-formed questions, and remarked, "I guess divorce can make a victim out of a child. I've often sensed a darker mood beneath Corey's happy-go-lucky flippancy. I guess this explains it."

"I try to be objective about it and remember he had a rough time growing up," T.K. said, his voice thinning to an emotionless monotone. "His father was a decent sort. He loved him I'm sure, or he wouldn't have fought so desperately for his custody. Grand-dad later told me the only way he won, was that Mother didn't want Corey as a burden to a new marriage.

"Anyway, Corey's father was an unskilled laborer. He barely earned enough to make ends meet. But he had a stiff-necked pride that disallowed taking a penny from my mother, who could well afford it, for Corey's support. He wouldn't let her lavish gifts on Corey either. Not even on birthdays or Christmas. She used to get really irate over it."

His eyes were distant as he gazed out over the lake and continued. "Legally, Mother was entitled to visitation rights. Beyond that Corey's father made no concessions. I've since thought Corey'd have been better off if Mother had remained out of his life completely. As it was, Corey bounced back and forth between near poverty with his father to opulence one day every week with my mother."

His laugh was harsh and grating. Mandy caught her lip, distressed for him, and yes, for Corey too, as he continued.

"To him, I represented the 'Haves' and he had no doubt but that he was a 'Have-not'. I guess he must have hated my guts from the time I was in diapers on. But because I was several years younger than he, it took me a long time to see it."

A long silence ran between them, Mandy gradually waking up to the realization that, as far as he was concerned, the explanation was over.

Clinging to a remnant of hope that brotherhood could be salvaged despite what had gone before, Mandy ventured, "Maybe you're wrong about him hating you, T.K. If he hated you, would he be your partner?"

Words self-deriding, he said, "That was my one attempt at reconciliation. A mass failure, I might add. The opportunist in Corey accepted the windfall chance at playing the big-shot. But cynic that he is, he regarded it as an attempt on my part to buy off his hostilities. No, if anything, I made matters worse by investing my inheritance from Mother in a business we could co-own."

His words rendered incorrect her assumption that Corey had, by his ambition and drive, worked into his current position at Four Seasons. Seeing T.K.'s generous gesture for what it was, she now understood the covetous look she'd surprised in his eyes several times over the weekend.

In his heart, beneath the pride, he'd like nothing better than to have a brother he could relate to as she related to Ellen. To him, it had nothing to do with wealth or power. It was the basic human need for a close family unit. Apparently, he'd lacked that. It also explained why the old victorian mansion which sparked such pride in Mrs. Hart left him cold. Why he derived more pleasure from time spent with his grandfather and his dogs than time spent building up his company. Why he'd once told her money was not a barrier between them. To him, it wasn't. For the first time since she'd realized the extent of his wealth and position, her heart beat with faint hope. If the simple things in life like love and family were high on his priorities, maybe she stood a chance after all. Maybe someday he would come to love her as she loved him.

He stirred one oar in the water, though his eyes were on her. "Now that you see where things stand between Corey and I, you'll better understand what I want of you. I know I have no right to ask, but I'm going to ask anyway on the grounds that you're special to me and I have to know in whose camp you stand."

He needed go no further. Her heart quaked as she met the raw yearning in his eyes and interpreted his silent appeal for a show of loyalty. She wanted nothing more than to give it to him. But what of Corey? Did she shut him out like a disposable friend? Did she forget the burden she felt on her heart for him when just this morning, after reflecting upon the sermon, she'd resolved to do something about that burden? Now, when it was more evident than ever Corey needed to be told there was Someone who loved him enough to alleviate all the hurt he'd endured through the long ago break-up of his family, did she turn her back on that need? Or did she keep their friendship secure so she could let her light shine?

Almost pleadingly, she said, "T.K., Corey's never been more than a friend to me."

"You've said that before and I believe you. But

there is something you must understand. Corey isn't aware I've been seeing you. At least, I haven't told him."

She shook her head at his inquiring glance, indicating she hadn't told him either, though it was in the back of her mind that Ellen had.

"In his eyes, I'm still the rich kid who gets all the breaks," T.K. went on, voice bereft of emotion. "He sports a competitive streak where I'm concerned that borders on fanatic. There have been other girls . . ."

Letting the sentence drift, he turned the boat and paddled with an expenditure of energy that spoke of pent-up emotions. "It never mattered before," he said gruffly. "But it matters now. I want you to stay as far from him as you possibly can."

He didn't say "Will you?" or "Can I have your word on that?" Nor did she give it. But she had a strong feeling their relationship weighed in the balance.

It was a sobering thought to accompany her home after such an idyllic weekend.

CHAPTER 10

As GOOD AS IT was to be home again, Mandy sighed as she picked a dead leaf off her favorite houseplant. She missed T.K. already, which was silly, for he'd gone with the promise to return as soon as he'd unpacked and checked on his grandfather.

Instead of floating around on a cloud of daydreams, she ought to be bathing and making preparations for the late dinner she'd guaranteed him.

Humming to herself, Mandy slipped in and out of a warm tub of fragrant bubbles, dressed in a lilac sleeveless wrap-around dress, then put pork chops on to fry.

Dinner was waiting on low burners when a loud knock brought Mandy up short. Corey! Anyone else would ring the bell. She finished setting the table, seriously considering not answering the door.

And what did she hope to accomplish by cowering in the kitchen, her common sense scolded as the knock was repeated with a ring of insistence.

Heart heavy with foreboding, Mandy answered the door and tried to summon a natural smile. "Hello, Corey."

Face a mask of tight lines, he stepped inside and closed the door. "You and Tommy enjoy your secluded weekend at the lake?" he asked, his voice an insulting jeer.

Mandy blushed hot at his implication. Tilting her chin, she returned mildly, "Yes, T.K. and I had a nice weekend, but it wasn't secluded. If you'd checked out the facts before you started slinging mud, you'd know that Ellen and Gregory went with us."

"The lake house is big. I doubt your privacy was infringed upon," he said, voice frigid.

Mandy opened her mouth to correct his misconception, then closed it again as he added, "I'm a little surprised at Ellen, putting the cart before the horse, so to speak. I thought she had better sense. But, then, at least she's only a week away from the altar.

"As for you, I hate to admit it, but you've had me fooled. I had you pegged as one girl who didn't mess around. I see now I was wrong. That kind of girl must not exist any longer." His eyes roved her figure offensively. "I wish I'd known sooner. We could have had some memorable times."

Cringing at his barbed remarks, Mandy stood her ground. "You're mistaken Corey. We didn't spend the weekend at the lake house, nor did we spend it together in the way you're implying."

"My, how you can lie!" He gave her a wintry smile. "If I hadn't seen you there with my own eyes, you'd almost convince me with that air of innocence."

"You couldn't have seen . . ." Mandy stopped short, mind flashing back to a moment in the rowboat when T.K. had looked toward the A-frame house and remarked he felt like they were being watched.

"I'm beginning to understand," she said. "You saw us out on the lake in the rowboat. And from there, you jumped to the conclusion that . . ."

"Conclusion, nothing!" he interrupted, eyes blazing. "You've played a fine game, Mand. Almost had me believing there was something to that Christianity of yours. How you and Tommy must have laughed at me!"

"No one laughed at you, Corey." She drew a ragged breath, mind considering two separate methods of dealing with him. She could keep silent and let him believe whatever he pleased. It would end their association and solve the problem of T.K.'s request for unconditional loyalty.

The other road was more difficult and offered no guarantee of accomplishing anything positive. She could try to convince him of the truth, salvage their friendship, and keep the door of communication open. How else could she be free of this burden? She couldn't. Not until she'd shown him that God could be the answer for him, as He was the answer for many who'd suffered at the hands of broken homes and relationships.

The disillusionment in his tortured gaze moved her to compassion and drained her of all anger. She lay a gentle hand on his arm.

"Corey, I'm going to tell you once more you're mistaken, then let it go at that. People tend to believe pretty much what they want to believe anyway."

His face a conflict of emotions—hurt, anger, and yes, a ray of hope—Corey said harshly, "I want to believe you, Mand. But I don't want to walk away feeling duped. I saw you out at the lake."

"We *were* out at the lake," she said, "but only long enough to take a ride in the row boat. Ellen and I shared a room at a motel this past weekend," she added, so there could be no misunderstanding unless he simply chose to think the worst of her.

"Maybe," she went on, watching his face work through the struggle of believing her, "Ellen and I used poor judgment. Maybe we shouldn't have gone at all. But my conscience is clean, so I'm not going to apologize for going to Branson with your brother."

160

His eyes reflected surprise, then anger. "He told you?"

"Yes, he told me. And I can't imagine why you've kept it such a secret. He's a brother to inspire pride. You shouldn't treat him like a skeleton in a dark closet."

Mandy backed against the door as he exploded into an outflow of bitter curses. She shut her eyes as he clenched his fists and hit the door on both sides of her face so hard, her head felt the vibrations of the blows against the solid wood and the sound of it reverberated through the small apartment.

"Don't stand there and tell me what a wonder he is!" he shouted, voice raw with rage. "I don't want to hear it!"

Mandy opened her eyes, praying for calm in the face of his malignant hatred for T.K.

"All my life, I had to listen to it from my mother. Tommy and his high marks at school. Tommy and his ability as an athlete. Tommy on the student council. 'Why can't you be more like Tommy?' she'd ask, until the very sound of his name made me sick to my stomach!" he spat.

"Everything I had to battle for, Tommy had served up on a golden platter. Someday, I kept telling myself, things will even up. Someday I'll achieve something, *anything*, just to make my mother proud.

"But she died before I could make it happen. It wasn't bad enough Tommy took her love from me in life. He took it in death too. She left every thin dime to him!"

Eyes glinting malice, he ground out, "The crowning insult was if any of the inheritance was to be mine, I had to accept it like common charity from a brother I'd spent my life loathing. I took it, darn right, I took it! And I vowed I'd dedicate every day of my life reminding the mighty Thomas Kyle Cooke the debt was no more than what he owed me for having spent my life in his shadow."

161

"He owed you no debt, Corey," Mandy said quietly, a peace flowing over her as she undertook the burden God had put upon her heart. "I don't know the trials of your childhood, nor do I need to, because whatever they were, Jesus is the answer. No!" she said, when he tried to interrupt. "I listened to you, now it's my turn!"

Struggling to find the right words, Mandy looked into his stormy eyes. "T.K. wasn't offering you charity by making you an equal partner in Four Seasons. He was wanting to mend a broken relationship. Perhaps it was foolish of him to think he could do it in that way, for the only true healer of bitterness and hatred is Christ Jesus."

"You don't know what you're talking about," Corey said, voice weary beyond belief. "What can you know of bitterness and hatred? You've always had the love of a close-knit family."

"You can too, Corey. There is no relationship any closer than the relationship you can have with Jesus. For a long time, I've been wanting to tell you that, but I've lacked the courage. But now I see how badly you need to be told and I'm no longer afraid of what you might think or say. The simple truth is, there is one who loves you enough to heal all hurt. He loved you enough to die for you."

"No one could love another that much. It's a dog-eat-dog world, Mand. Each man for himself." Corey's flippancy returned, though in the depths of his eyes there was a bleak sadness.

"It's that way only when we allow it to be. T.K. wasn't dog-eat-dog with you," she risked making the point. "He wasn't compelled to share his inheritance."

Corey said nothing in return, only hardened his face against the name of his brother. The phone rang, breaking the silence between them. Mandy said, as she went to answer it,

"I can't force-feed you what Christ has to offer, Corey. He Himself won't trespass. You have to ask him into your heart, to renew your life. All I can do is hope you'll think about it. I'll pray for you too and be here if you have questions, or simply need to talk."

It was Miss Princeton on the phone, upset because Willie was playing tag on the stairway between the first and second floor of the building. The normalcy of the request she was about to make yanked Mandy out of the deep vacuum she'd fallen into.

"Every time I get within a few feet of him, he dashes up a couple more steps," her elderly neighbor complained, her breath coming in short, winded gasps. "I hate to ask, but your legs are much younger than mine. Do you think you could catch him for me?"

Agreeing to come right away, Mandy hung up the phone and turned back to Corey. "I'll be right back. Willie's playing tricks on Miss Princeton again."

He caught her hand before she could open the door. Chaffing it between his two hands, he said, "You're a good little Samaritan, Mand. Just the kind of girl I've always wanted to marry. Would they de-church you if you married a hapless character like me?"

Half-smiling at the word he'd coined, she pulled her hand away. "Corey, I'm fond of you, but . . ."

"Don't repeat that brotherly-sisterly stuff," he said, brushing the words from her lips with a light kiss. "Give me some time to get my act together. I'll start going to church with you, maybe even dust off the old Bible. Will that satisfy you, Mand. Bring me up to snuff?"

"Corey, I don't want you to do it for me, I want you to do it for *you*."

"I know. That's just what makes you so special. You care without any reason to." He would have kissed her again, but she jumped out of reach, her heart knocking a fatal beat at the sound of the doorbell.

It would be T.K. right on time for their late dinner. For one wild moment, she felt the crazy temptation to hide Corey in the closet or beg him to crawl out the window, like in some mad-cap comedy. But this was real life, and she would have to face T.K.'s almost certain anger at finding Corey in her apartment only hours after asking her for a show of unconditional loyalty.

Her hand on the door, Mandy heard herself say, "That will be T.K. I want to talk to him alone a minute, Corey, if you'll excuse me."

She slipped out and closed the door behind her. T.K. met her with a heart-tugging grin, the grey-stripe of his knit shirt accenting the grey gleam in his eyes.

"Aren't you going to invite me in?" He stooped to kiss her cheek. "You smell nice. Is that perfume or dinner?"

"Corey's here." She forced the words out, hating the blunt sound of them and what they did to T.K.'s warmth. He straightened, took a step back and gave her a long thorough look. "I see."

"No, you probably don't." She sighed deeply. "I'll explain later. But for now, would you promise you'll be nice? I know it's awkward, but I can't just tell him to leave."

"You surely haven't invited him to stay." Tension charged the air between them. "Mandy, I thought we had this all sorted out this afternoon."

"I don't think you realize what you're asking of me, T.K. Corey and I have been friends a long time. It isn't normal just to shut him out all at once." Her pulse throbbed a hollow beat in her throat as she met his hard look.

"These aren't normal circumstances," T.K. argued. "I said I knew it wasn't fair of me to ask, but because I thought we had something special, something we didn't want to risk losing, I asked."

"We *do* have something special." Mandy chewed

on her bottom lip, desperate to find the words he would understand. "But it would be like my asking you to fire Miss Thomas, point blank, no explanations given. How would that make you feel?"

"She isn't *my* secretary. She's Corey's." He frowned darkly, purposely obtuse.

"Then Mrs. Hart," Mandy supplied another example. "You wouldn't want to fire Mrs. Hart just because I wanted you to."

"Mandy, that's different. That hasn't anything to do with you. Your relationship with Corey has a lot to do with me."

She could not mistake the threat in his voice, yet neither could she back down on her promise to Corey. She'd said she'd be there when he needed to talk, and she would. If only T.K. could see that the hard feelings between him and his brother needed not go on if both would try to begin anew.

"I know I'm way out of my depth here," she fumbled for words. "But it seems to me it's time you and Corey put the past behind you. He isn't a bad person, T.K. And he's bearing some bitter scars.

"We had a long talk. He told me he'd always felt as if he were second rate in your mother's eyes. T.K., that couldn't have been easy."

T.K. gave a disgusted snort. "Mandy, he'd say anything to get your sympathy. He lies as easy as he breathes. Forgive me if I remain unmoved by his rejected kid story, but it's a repeat performance, as far as I'm concerned."

"I think he was serious."

"I don't much appreciate your taking his side." The lines of T.K.'s mouth were set grim and harsh against anything she might say.

Nonetheless, she denied it. "I'm not taking sides. I'm saying, does there have to *be* sides?"

A muscle along his jawline flexed, the silence between them ominous. Down the hallway, the

165

stairwell door opened. Miss Princeton came into view, her quavery cry of relief interrupting the tension.

"Mandy! Thank goodness. That Willie is such a bad boy. Oh, but he's going to be sorry!" the old lady bristled as she shuffled toward her apartment. "Just let me get a bite of tuna and we'll see if we can't lure him into captivity. Then I promise, I shan't let him out of my apartment ever again."

Mandy turned beseeching eyes upon T.K. "I told her I'd help her catch Willie. T.K., go on in. Sit down and talk to Corey. That isn't asking too much, is it? You can talk business, or anything neutral. You don't have to get on shaky ground."

Grave-faced, he gave a truculent nod and swung her door open to disappear inside. Mandy let out a lung full of air and went to capture Willie. Using tuna as bait, it didn't take long. But upon returning to her apartment, she was immediately hit with a feeling of trepidation.

From the kitchen she heard the sounds of Corey singing off key as he dished up dinner. The dinner she'd prepared for T.K. And T.K? He was nowhere to be seen.

CHAPTER 11

MANDY HOVERED IN THE doorway of the kitchen, heart pounding with dread. "Where's T.K.?"

Corey turned and flashed her a sardonic grin as he put a bowl of vegetables on the table. "Tommy left in a huff. No need wasting good food, though. I've invited myself in his stead. Let's sit down and dig in before it gets cold."

Mandy stood motionless, as stunned by the change in Corey as she was by the bruise taking shape along his jaw. "Good land Corey, what happened?"

"Hmm?" He put a hot-pad under the dish, then touched his face. "Oh, *this*," he feigned a nonchalance he couldn't possibly feel. "Let's just say I brought out the latent beast in Tommy. Never did believe he was as civilized as he pretended."

"T.K. *hit you?*" her voice reached a shrill note.

"As a matter of fact, he did." He took a place at the table and gingerly touched his jaw again.

Mandy scurried to the sink, dampened a cloth and wrapped an icecube in it. Applying it to his face, she cried, "Is anything broken?"

"No, I don't think so." He winced. "That hurts. No, don't stop. It's worth a little pain, being doctored by you."

Mandy slammed the wash cloth down on the table and backed away from the arms that reached out to hold her. "Corey, you'd better tell me right now what has been going on! What did you say to make T.K. hit you? And don't try to tell me you didn't provoke it because I won't believe you!"

"Simmer down, Mand. I didn't say anything to him I hadn't already said to you. Or do you want it verbatim?" A glint in his eye, he opened his mouth to proceed.

"Please, just spare me!" She sank into a chair and buried her face in her hands.

"I might add, he didn't take my accusations nearly so well as you," he said.

Her head shot up. "What's the matter with you, Corey? You act like it was a privilege getting socked on the jaw? Aren't you mad?"

"If that was the price I had to pay to see you were telling me the truth, that nothing happened between you and Tommy this weekend, then I guess it was a decent trade-off."

"I already *told* you nothing happened!"

"I know. And I wanted to believe you, but a woman like you would naturally lie about something like that. I'm relatively certain, though, Tommy wasn't lying," he said dryly, and stroked his jaw again. "He backed up his denial with a pretty rough punch and a colorful description of what he'd do to me if I ever said anything like that about you again."

His mouth twisted in a wry grin. "Without intending to, he reassured me I hadn't lost you yet, Mand."

Mandy threw her hands up in dismay. "You're impossible! What am I supposed to do with you?"

"Treat me kindly." He laughed at her look of outrage and began to fill her plate.

168

The meal she'd so lovingly prepared had about the same appeal as Willie's dry cat food. While she moved it around her plate, wondering if the damage done to her relationship with T.K. was irreparable, the lump in her throat grew and grew.

Corey, on the other hand, seemed unbothered by the darkening bruise on his jaw. He ate with great relish, complimenting her on her cooking and helping himself to seconds. Finally, he complained,

"You aren't eating."

She offered no explanation, just tossed down her fork and flung her wadded napkin onto the table.

A sigh shook loose from Corey's lungs. "It isn't going to work, is it?"

Mandy roused herself enough to ask, "What isn't going to work?"

"Us." His eyes flickered regret. "I have lost you after all. You love him, don't you?"

Mutely, Mandy confessed it with a scant nod. A hot tear stole down her cheek. She averted her face to hide it. She couldn't have said exactly when he left, but when she lifted her head again, she was alone.

A night had never felt so lonely. Or the day after so long and empty. The ache in her heart was multiplied by the silence of the phone.

Surely T.K. would call, Mandy thought for the hundredth time as afternoon gave way to early evening. Surely she meant enough to him, he'd take the trouble to dial her number so they could talk things through. All along, hadn't he been the one for talking things through, for straightening out misunderstandings so their relationship could grow?

Intent on keeping busy, Mandy loaded her soiled clothes into a large basket and went to the wash room in the basement of her building.

Going through the mechanics of separating her wash into three different machines, Mandy came across the sun-dress she'd worn when they'd gone rowing. As she pressed it into the machine, the faint woodsy scent of T.K.'s after-shave wafted to her nose. Swallowing a sob, she unloaded the machines and stuffed all the dirty clothes into her basket again.

All this suffering, and why? she demanded of herself.

Ignoring the strange look she received from a lady in outrageous purple hair-rollers, Mandy swung out the door and up the stairs. T.K. was a reasonable man, she told herself. He wasn't given to rash, temperamental behavior. He'd been upset last night, but by now he'd had time to think it over.

She would drive out to his place and they would talk. Even if the very worst happened and he told her it was over between them, it would be more bearable than every minute hinging on a phone call that might never come.

The road out seemed so sweetly familiar. She had missed going to the lodge. The varying shades of green along the country road had a tranquilizing influence on her troubled mind and she arrived at T.K.'s country estate feeling more hope than she had all day.

However, on her way to the front door, it suddenly occurred to her she hadn't the faintest idea what she was going to say. To her relief, it was Mrs. Hart who answered the door.

"Hello, Mrs. Hart," she said, and tried to smile past her trepidation. "Is T.K. here?"

Mrs. Hart swung the door open wide and invited her in. "Thomas is down at the kennels. But I'll send his grandfather after him. Why don't you step into the parlor to wait?"

"No, don't bother Kyle. I'll go to the kennels myself," Mandy said before her courage could give way.

The path leading to the kennels was down-hill, tree-shrouded and well-traveled. The building over the

170

kennels seemed to spring out of the ground in an otherwise wilderness area. Two sides of the building opened via sliding track doors to allow light and ventilation.

Mandy glanced at the mesh wire cages and long narrow runs. T.K. had his back to her as he opened one cage and slid dishes of food and fresh water inside.

The sight of his plaid shirt stretching across broad shoulders, his lean waist and trim, jean-clad hips went over her like a soothing balm. His voice was soft as he spoke to the dog within the enclosure, fondling her ears. She took a long, steadying breath. Surely everything could be made right.

Seeming to sense her presence, he turned. The spontaneous welcome which leaped to his eyes was so quickly extinguished she decided with a plummeting heart wishful thinking had imagined it so.

"What are you doing here?" He closed the cage and turned to face her.

Her painted-on smile went out at his brusque tone. She said, "You invited me. Remember? To see the pups."

"Oh, the pups, is it?" He flipped the catch on the next cage and lifted out a puppy. "Any pup will do I suppose, as long as it proves your point."

The gentleness of his hands cupping the puppy seemed a contradiction to his harsh expression. She swallowed hard. "My point?"

He deposited the puppy into her awaiting hands. "Selfless bravery in the face of this snarling, man-eating creature."

Had he smiled, or had his tone been less sarcastic, she might have laughed and answered in like vein. But he did not smile and his eyes as they regarded her were cynical.

Unable to bear his harsh scrutiny, she tried to blank him out and think only of the puppy until she could collect her composure. His fur was soft and warm, a baby-whimper rumbled in his throat and his tiny tongue was soft and wet upon her face. Fear of such a helpless little creature would have been absurd. Mandy stroked him with her fingers.

"Therapy's over," T.K. said abruptly and reached for the pup. "His mother's getting nervous. Must sense your hostilities."

It wasn't like him to be so cutting. Her heart throbbed with pain, and her voice came out very small. "T.K., can we talk?"

"I don't see we have anything to say to one another."

It took him a moment to secure the cage. She tried desperately to hide her ragged feelings behind a calm, "T.K., I know you're angry, but if we could just work it out . . ."

"I was ready to work it out last night," he interrupted curtly. "But you didn't seem to have the time between your neighbor's cat and Corey."

"I spent five minutes getting that cat," she bit off in self-defense. "Surely you could have waited five minutes without slugging Corey and taking off in a huff."

"It bothers you doesn't it, that I slugged poor, misunderstood Corey? If you're wanting me to say I'm sorry, forget it. I'm not. He deserved it and if I had it to do over, I'd make it a better punch."

"Why, you're jealous!" surprise wrung the words from her.

"Darn right, I'm jealous. I think a guy has a right to expect a little loyalty from a girl whose made a pretty good show of caring about him."

Intimidated by the taut set of his mouth and his narrowed eyes, Mandy admitted in a strained whisper, "I do care. And I wasn't disloyal."

"Weren't you? Then maybe you'd better reexamine your definition of the word. How long does it take to tell an ex-boyfriend to hit the road, there's someone new in your life?''

He towered so near, the rigid lines of his face reminding her again of a proud warrior, only now, a warrior striking out to extract his revenge. If he felt he needed to redeem his honor, then so be it. She would have plucked her eyes out sooner than show the weakness of tears.

Stonily she repeated the tiresome words, "Corey has never been more than a friend.''

"You keep telling me that, but I find it harder and harder to believe,'' he said with a cool demeanor. "I drove around awhile last evening, then came back to your apartment. It'd been half an hour, maybe longer. Corey's car was still in the lot. I waited another fifteen minutes. No sign of him leaving. I would think even your Miss Princeton would have begun to get suspicious by that time.''

His eyes, as grey and hard as steel, held hers in a clashing of accusations and silent denials. If he loved her, he would not be so unapproachable, so hard-headed and determined to inflict hurt. She'd been humming a pipedream, thinking what ran between them was strong enough to endure. He'd stripped her of her pride and robbed her of her dream, but darned if she'd go down on her knees and plead forgiveness when she'd done nothing but what she felt was right.

Slowly, she turned and walked away. Behind her she heard his swift intake of breath and dared for a moment to hope he'd call her back. But he didn't. Nor did he follow.

She drove as far as the lodge turn-off when the tears became blinding. Turning up the road, crossing the crude bridge, she came to a stop in front of the lodge.

She walked to the red oak, sank down on her heels and cried her heart out. A long while later, when darkness turned the hills into a land of shadows, she drove back to town, vowing never to cry over T.K. Cooke again.

It was a vow intolerably hard to keep in coming days. Ellen's last minute flurry of wedding plans was a constant reminder there would be no wedding for her. The realization was a bitter one, for she'd always thought sometime in her life there would be a marriage and children. But her love for T.K. had gone deep, so deep she was certain she'd never love again.

At times it was a temptation to blame Corey in part for the misery she was enduring. Yet to resent him would have been as futile as her dread of dogs had been in the aftermath of her mother's death. Anyway, Corey was nowhere around to blame. She hadn't seen him since the evening he'd invited himself to stay for supper at her apartment. Was it wicked of her to be thankful he was absent from her life now?

Not wanting to think it through, Mandy masked her broken heart behind an overly bright smile and plunged in devotedly to helping Ellen's wedding day be all it could be.

Gram, if surprised, was openly grateful for her all but taking over responsibility for the reception. Early Friday morning, Mandy drove to her father's house to attend to last minutes chores. After stringing colored lanterns around the patio and setting up tables and chairs, she turned to the final grooming of the weeping willow tree.

Ellen had her heart set on yellow ribbons adorning the tree. So perched atop a shaky ladder, Mandy tied ribbon after ribbon.

Mid-morning, Gram came to the back door and called, "Phone, Mandy. A Mr. Cooke, I believe he said."

Heart swelling with hope, Mandy toppled the ladder and banged her shins in her rush to reach the phone. Then, she came crashing back to earth, for the voice on the line belonged to Kyle, not T.K.

"You're a hard girl to track down. I couldn't remember your father's name, so I tried every Holt in

174

the book." Kyle laughed his throaty laugh. "Been missing me?"

"Sure I have, Kyle." She worked down the last of her disappointment.

"Good," he said. "Then maybe you'll agree to fittin' me into your schedule today. Say about noon? I'd even let you twist my arm into eating a sandwich with you."

Touched by the plea in his voice, Mandy said, "I'd like to Kyle, but today is Ellen's wedding day. I don't have the time to run out."

"Oh, I wasn't wantin' you to," he said quickly. "Mrs. Hart'll be leaving any time now for her day off and the boy isn't due home until early evening. So I'm at loose ends. I was thinking I'd run into town to see you. I won't take but a few minutes of your time."

Mandy paused a second, mentally working through the day. The church ladies would be bringing in salads and sandwiches for the reception which they would serve after the wedding. She didn't have to be at the church before six, so actually, things were very well under control.

"All right, Kyle. I plan to be here at my father's for the rest of the day. Let me give you the address. And Kyle? Come hungry. My Gram is some kind of a cook."

He cackled as he took directions down, then assured her he'd be there by noon. Mandy went out and finished tying the yellow ribbons onto the willow tree, washed down the patio and driveway, then fussed around pulling dead blooms off flowers until noon when Ellen returned from the hairdresser. Her face glowed beneath the crowning halo of her golden hair, and she was every inch the happy bride-to-be.

Twelve-thirty came and went without any sign of Kyle. Curious to know why the delay, Mandy rang his number, but there was no answer. Reasoning he was on his way, she went upstairs and helped Ellen pack for her honeymoon in St. Louis.

At one, she and Ellen and Gram broke down and ate without Kyle. Her father said he wasn't hungry and they teased him about being nervous until he went into the study and closed the door, complaining about "women-folk." A while later the minister phoned to say the church sanctuary had been decorated with flowers and candles and everything was in readiness.

Mandy had begun to worry in earnest. Surely Kyle would have phoned if he'd decided not to come. Could he have had trouble on the road. That truck he drove was a rickety old thing. By two o'clock everyone in the house knew she was worried.

Her father, who'd come out of the study complaining he was hungry told her to relax. "He'll get here when he gets here."

"Mandy stop pacing, you'll wear a hole in the rug," Gram said, peering over her glasses.

Ellen said pointedly, "I've been calm all day, and now you're making me nervous."

"I can't help it!" Mandy said. "He's a dependable old guy. I can't imagine what's happened to him. Maybe I should run out and check up on him. He could be stalled along the road."

"Mandy, I'm sure that isn't necessary," her father said, but Ellen interrupted.

"Let her go. She isn't going to settle down until she knows he's fine."

Mandy caught up her pocketbook and gave Ellen a hug. "I'll be right back Ellen, I promise. It's a fifteen minute drive out, so I've loads of time."

"Just get going," Ellen ordered, then under her breath, "If she delays my wedding, I'm going to make myself an only child."

Mandy made the drive in record speed, watching the roadside all along the way without any sign of Kyle's old pick-up truck. However, upon coming to the end of the tree-lined drive, she saw it parked in a shady spot.

Misgivings growing, she climbed the veranda steps and leaned on the bell. Immediately a deep-throated bark sounded, followed a few seconds later, by the scratching of a dog's paws on the other side of the door.

Heart in her throat, she backed away from the door, expecting Kyle to fling it open and the dog to bound out at her. But that didn't happen. She rang the bell again and the urgency of the dog's bark increased. What on earth? she wondered, waiting a full five minutes, and ringing the bell intermittently. All sorts of awful thoughts entered her mind.

Surely Kyle was inside. Feeling like an intruder, she walked along the screened-in veranda, peering in windows. The open porch ran on around to the south side of the house. Mandy continued down it, still glancing in for some sign of Kyle. Recognizing the parlor furniture, she stopped short. Her heart leaped to her throat as she spotted on the floor two overall-clad legs extending from beyond the camel-back sofa.

"Kyle!" She rapped on the window. Though there was no reply, it seemed to her his left foot moved. If only the sofa wasn't blocking the rest of his body from view!

She flew around to the front door again, then hesitated, frightened at what the reaction of the dog would be if she opened the door. As it was, his barking bordered on frantic. Old memories rose up to haunt her. With an unsteady hand, she reached for the door knob. Maybe she should simply go for help. Her courage wavered. But no! Kyle could be dying even now as she hesitated. Every second could be of vital importance. Simultaneously, a prayer and an hysterical sob caught at her throat. She'd prayed for the removal of her fears. But never had she dreamed there would come so critical a testing as this. Her fingers clutched the door-knob and turned. She squeezed her eyes shut tight as the dog leaped out at her.

"Down! You get down!" she shrieked, and the dog dropped down to the porch floor. Her heart dared beat again as she recognized the freckled chest of Kyle's shadow, Clancy.

He kept up his barking, though his mouth was frothy and his tongue hung out like a limp, wet piece of leather. Mandy gritted her teeth and made herself pat him on the head to assure him she meant no harm. Then, stepping past him, she went to the parlor, the dog at her heels.

Kyle was on his side, his face pasty white and one leg twisted at an odd angle. Kneeling beside him, Mandy found a strong pulse and nearly wept in relief.

"Kyle?" she spoke softly so as not to alarm him. "It's me, Mandy. Here, let me put this pillow under your head," she said, yanking one off the sofa. "There, that's better. Now, lay still. I'm going to call an ambulance."

His eyes flickered open and focused on her as if from a great distance. He parted his lips, but Mandy hushed him. "Save your strength. Oh Lord, where's the phone book?" she muttered, scrambling through a drawer of the phone table.

Her trembling hands settled upon it, then whipped through pages seeking the hospital ambulance service. By the time she'd completed the call, Kyle seemed more alert. Sitting on the floor beside him, she took his hand.

"It's going to be all right, Kyle. The ambulance will be here in no time. Just rest easy."

Clancy sat on his haunches beside her whining softly and stretching out to lick Kyle's face from time to time. Kyle winced and grumbled, "Stow the kisses, Clancy. I'm not forgettin' it was you who got tangled up in my feet."

Never had Mandy seen a better description of "hang-dog." Clancy dropped down and buried his head between his paws with a pitiful whine. Moved to pity, she gave his head a second reluctant pat.

"It's okay, Clancy. He's going to be okay."

"Leg's busted, Mandy. I know it is," Kyle pushed the words between pale lips. "It's hard on an old codger like me."

Tears stung her eyes. "I know, Kyle. But it won't be long now. Don't try to talk."

"Have to," he said, his breathing becoming shallow. "The boy ain't been himself lately and I want you to tell me why. That's the reason I was coming to see you, only Clancy got in the way and I didn't make it."

"Kyle . . ." she protested.

"No beating around the bush. Ain't time. Have you two quarrelled?" he demanded, his faded eyes holding her miserable gaze.

She admitted it with a brief nod.

"Bet it was over Corey, wasn't it?"

Mandy was startled into asking, "How'd you know?"

"Wasn't hard to figure. Every time T.K. gets a gal he cares anything about, Corey comes along and messes it up. One time he went so far as to call this girl T.K.'d been datin' and asking her did she know Thomas Kyle Cooke was being investigated by the FBI for possible underworld connections."

A quirk of a grin twisted her mouth despite the stern look Kyle turned on her. "He tell you some fish story like that about the boy?" he demanded.

"No, Kyle. It wasn't anything Corey said."

"Then what's the trouble?"

Seeing nothing but the truth would satisfy him, Mandy poured out the whole story. When she'd finished, he lay so quiet, his eyes shut, she grabbed for his wrist and murmured, "Kyle? Are you all right?"

A weary sigh shook him. "Should have known it was something like this. You know, deep down, T.K.'d always wanted to get along with Corey. That's

179

why he shared his mother's money. I guess he felt guilty he'd grown up having so much when Corey had so little. But myself, I've never been sure Corey had it any rougher than T.K."

"Kyle! How can you say that? Corey must have had a miserable childhood, his mother casting him in T.K.'s shadow all the time and rejecting him, at least in his eyes."

"That's just it, Mandy. What Corey never realized is he was better off without his mother. He saw her once a week. T.K. put up with her every day. Now I don't like to speak ill of the dead, but doggone it, there isn't any good to be said of her. Mother-love wasn't in that woman. She turned Corey and T.K. against one another from the very beginning. I can't say what kind of kick it gave her. People like that, there's no understanding."

He was silent a while, sorting out his thoughts. When he spoke again, it was in an economy of phrases as his strength dwindled.

"T.K. didn't clean his room or eat his vegetables? She'd say he was spoiled, how'd he like to be Corey, didn't even have a room of his own. Sleeping on an old sofa. Eating canned spaghetti and frozen pizzas. Or if he ripped the knee out of his pants like boys do, it'd be he didn't appreciate anything she did for him. She ought to pack up everything he owned and give it to Corey."

The sickness of it curled her stomach and filled her with a quiet rage. How could a mother be so cruel, pitting her sons against one another in that way? And T.K., never saying a word against her! No wonder he'd been hurt and angry thinking she'd taken Corey's part. Just as it must have seemed his mother had done in the years they were growing up.

"My boy, T.K.'s father," Kyle continued weakly, "he was too tied up in his profession to see it clearly until T.K. got bigger. Much as I loved him, Thomas wasn't much for standing up to his wife. The only thing he did against her will was let me see all I wanted of T.K.''

"And you tried to undo all the damage his mother had done, didn't you?" She stooped to kiss his hot dry brow. "Bless you, Kyle, if I wasn't in love with another man, I'd ask you to marry me."

That seemed to please and reassure him, for he used up the last of his strength cackling. His blue-veined eyelids came down and with a shot of pure terror, Mandy felt his pulse again. Thank God, it was steady. He'd simply lost concsiousness.

A few minutes later, the wail of the ambulance siren roused him again. His eyes fluttered open as the white-coated attendants lifted him onto the gurney.

"I'll ride in with you," Mandy said.

"No." He shook his head. "The boy drove up-state this morning. He'll be back around supper time. Someone is going to have to be here to tell him and Mrs. Hart what happened. You'll stay, won't you?"

Because he implored her with tears in his eyes, Mandy agreed to stay. But once the sirens had faded she thought of Ellen's wedding and nearly cried out loud.

Ellen would never forgive her if she were to miss her wedding! She was maid of honor!

Clancy rubbed against her leg and stared up with soppy-sad eyes. She gave him a faint-hearted pat on the head and went to phone Ellen.

Having told her all about Kyle's accident, she promised, "I'll make it in time. If T.K. isn't home by six, I'll leave him a note. Gram can make certain my dress and shoes get to the church and all I'll have to do is throw them on."

"Mandy Holt, this is my wedding!" Ellen wailed. "You had better allow more time than just enough to 'throw' your clothes on! I want you here by five and not a minute later. There's a million buttons down the

181

back of my dress and I want you to do them up and . . ."

Mandy quietly put the phone back on the hook and prayed someone on the other end would calm down poor Ellen.

The waiting was hard. The old house seemed so silent and empty and for a while Clancy seemed questionable company. Not having been around dogs for such a long time, it was hard to get used to him even though the fear was gone. He kept edging closer and closer to her. Under any other circumstances, she might have shunned him. But he looked so sad-eyed and anxious, it finally got to her.

Her fingers edged down to rest upon his silky head. He licked her hand. After a while, like a child feeling his way along, he jumped up on the sofa beside her and gave her an inquiring look.

"Mrs. Hart wouldn't like this," Mandy scolded. But she relented and scratched his ears. To her surprise, she found comfort in his closeness and she raised no objections when he lay his head in her lap, closed his eyes and released deep dog sighs.

Perhaps it was inevitable her recent troubled nights would catch up with her. Repeated yawns and heavy eyes made it hard to keep alert. Thinking "Only for a moment or two," she gave in to the temptation and closed her eyes.

Whether it was the clock chiming five or the dog springing to the floor which awakened her, she couldn't have said. But when she opened her eyes, it was to find T.K. framed in the parlor door.

His dark suit jacket was hooked on one finger and flung back over his shoulder. His shirt was loose at the throat. But it was his expression that made her heart leap out of control. Before it could alter to hostility, Mandy bounded up from the sofa, blurting a brief explanation.

He didn't ask how she happened to find Kyle, only

how long it had been since they'd taken him and what kind of shape he'd been in when he left.

"I'm sure his leg was broken. He was beginning to slip in and out of consciousness." She swallowed hard, hurting for him. "T.K., I'm really sorry. If there's anything I can do, just let me know."

He accepted her offer with a brief nod, saying, "Thanks for staying." His eyes roamed her features and his lips remained parted as if there was more he had to say, but no words came.

Mandy stirred uneasily. "I have to get back to town. Ellen's going to be in a real dither. Her wedding, you know."

"Tonight?" He frowned. "You're looking kind of shaky. If you'll wait until I've changed clothes and fed the dogs, I'll drive you in on my way to the hospital."

Tempting though his offer was, she thought of Ellen and turned him down. "I'm all right, thanks anyway. But I would appreciate it if you'd let me know how Kyle's doing. I'll be at my father's house after the wedding. His number is in the book."

Nodding, he accompanied her as far as the front entryway, then turned aside to climb the carpeted stairway. Mandy let herself out and with a trembling heart, drove back to town.

Even now, it was hard to believe it really was over between them. Were the memories worth all the pain? The yearning she'd felt for his touch only moments ago was still fresh in her mind, a mind that shouted a resounding "No!"

But then she thought of their visit to the cave, the midnight swim, and the fun they'd had drifting from shop to shop in Branson. Maybe someday it would seem worth the price left to pay.

CHAPTER 12

ELLEN WAS A GORGEOUS, radiant bride, Gregory proud and handsome and Gram, bless her heart, cried a river of tears. The backyard reception, like the wedding proved a huge success.

Even after the bride and groom had taken their leave, many of the guests remained enjoying the food and drinks, the conversation, and the cool of the evening.

Tired to the bone, Mandy found a wrought-iron love-seat in a corner of the patio and sank down upon it, willing everyone to please go home.

"Antisocial in general, or is it me you're avoiding?"

Mandy lifted her gaze to find Corey standing before her, offering a cup of punch. Taking it, she made room for him on the seat, saying, "Just worn out. It's been a long day."

"So I heard. Your father mentioned something about old Kyle taking a fall. Pretty bad, was it?"

Questioning the sincerity of his interest, Mandy sipped her punch and took her time forming a reply. "I don't know, Corey. I was hoping T.K. would call and give me some word on how Kyle's doing. So far, he hasn't. I'm certain the leg was broken, but other than that, I couldn't tell you anything."

"Too bad." Corey gave his head a shake. "Old Kyle never had much use for me, but you know, I thought he was a pretty all right kind of guy. Even envied Tommy having a grand-dad like that."

Hand tightening on her punch cup, Mandy said, "Let's not get into that again, Corey. I'm not up to it."

"Hey, I wasn't trying to start anything. In fact, I've been giving some thought to a few things you said the other night. Might be some truth to it," he admitted briskly.

"To what?"

"Why, to the futility of Tommy and me hating each others guts," he said with perfect calm. "So I've decided to come clean and admit I've told you a few things about Tommy that aren't strictly true."

"Oh? What's that?" she asked guardedly.

"I told you he was a recluse? Remember? Before you'd ever met him?"

Mandy laughed in spite of herself. "Corey, you idiot. Don't you think I know him well enough by now to see that wasn't true?"

"It really wasn't such a big lie," he excused himself.

"No," she agreed sardonically. "Nothing at all compared to the FBI investigating him."

"You know about that?"

"Kyle told me."

Corey chuckled. "Once I told a girl he had a wife and three kids. She dropped Tommy like a hot potato and do you know, it didn't even make him mad? I did notice after that he was careful not to let it leak out who he was dating."

"You ought to be ashamed," Mandy chided, much to his amusement.

"So why the long face?" he asked abruptly. "You and Tommy still at odds over the other night?"

When she didn't answer, he tipped her face toward his and said, "Come on, Mand. Buck up. He'll come around."

She shook her head. Her bottom lip trembled. "We're pretty well quits."

Corey uttered a quiet oath. "If that's the way the wind blows, then I guess I'll have to have a talk with that pig-headed partner of mine."

"Corey, don't you dare! You'll only make things worse!"

"How much worse than quits can they be?" Ignoring her blustering protests, he chucked her on the chin. "Just leave it to me. If I can't have you, I might as well keep you in the family the only way I know how. Never let it be said I'm not a gracious loser."

She slumped against the back of the chair thinking what harm could come to a demolished relationship? Corey, at least, seemed to have recovered. He went on his way with a chipper salute back over his shoulder.

The party broke up soon after. Mandy sent Gram off to bed, changed into a pair of Ellen's jeans, and feet dragging, helped her father tackle the mess. It was well after eleven when they closed the door on the kitchen. Too tired to go home, she decided to spend the night in Ellen's bed.

Mandy was into Ellen's night-gown and combing out her hair, when the doorbell rang. She heard her father lumbering down the stairs, complaining under his breath. A moment later, he called up to her.

"Mandy? You still up? There's someone here to see you."

Certain it was Corey reporting back on his self-appointed mission as ambassador of peace, she grumbled as she pulled on the crumpled shirt and jeans again.

Bare feet took her halfway down the stairs before a familiar voice stopped her cold. It was T.K., not Corey at the foot of the stairs.

Lines of fatigue fanned out from his eyes. The skin seemed more tightly drawn across the fine, high ridge of his cheekbones. Even the straight masculine line of his mouth was set in weariness.

Heart galloping up to her throat, she tugged at her wrinkled shirt and took the remainder of the stairs before the words, "Hello, T.K.," would form on her lips. "How's Kyle?"

He ran a hand through rumpled hair. "It was a bad break. They put a pin in it. It's still early to tell, but the doctor seems to think he's in good shape for a man his age, and ought to regain full use of it."

If the reverse proved true and Kyle was unable to walk . . . No wonder T.K. looked so haggard! Compassion made it easier. Mandy reached for his hand.

"Come on into the living-room and sit down a while," she urged him. "Have you had anything to eat? There's plenty of sandwiches in the refrigerator. Dad? How about you? Would you like a cup of coffee?"

Her father yawned very broadly. "No thanks. The father of the bride is ready to call it a day." Extending his hand to T.K., he added, "I'm glad to hear your grandfather is holding his own. I'll trust Mandy to keep me posted on his progress." With another yawn, he called out a good-night and climbed the stairs again.

Alone with him now, Mandy felt suddenly shy and inadequate. "I'll get that sandwich," she murmured, angling off toward the kitchen.

He overtook her in one long stride. "The sandwich will wait. Talk to me first." He took her hand and pulled her along, refusing to release it even when he'd settled in her father's favorite chair.

She perched on the arm of the chair, half-dizzy with

187

his nearness, the warmth in his eyes, and the rough feel of his hand in hers.

"I tried to talk to Grand-dad," he began. "But he was pretty hazy on what had happened. Can you clear the picture up for me?"

Her pulse played leap-frog with her heart. Brushing at the tattered knee of her jeans with her free hand, she said, "Kyle called me this morning to say he was coming in to see me for a few minutes. He said he'd come around noon, but he never showed. I remembered you telling me when he said he'd do a thing, he did it, so when he hadn't come by two, I got worried and drove out there.

"He was on the parlor floor. I'm not sure how long he'd been there," she went on. "But he said he'd tripped over Clancy."

"Clancy. Now that's something that really had me puzzled," T.K. said, fingers trailing up the length of her arm and creating havoc with her heart. "He must have been raising an awful racket. He's so protective of Grand-dad. It must have taken a few years off your life, opening that door and marching in."

"I didn't march exactly. It was more like cowering on the veranda a moment, waiting for him to devour me." Her voice quivered as his hand reached the hollow of her throat to linger a moment before turning her face so her eyes were full on him. "When it became clear all he wanted was to get help, I went in and called an ambulance, and after a while, I realized I wasn't the least bit afraid of Clancy anymore."

"And why is that?" he asked, thumb tracing the curve of her cheek.

It was hard to keep her mind on her words. "I'm just not," she murmured, unwilling to tell him he was the reason.

His hand fell back to his knee then as he made an abrupt change of subject. "Corey came to the hospital to see Grand-dad. Decent of him, I have to admit, since Grand-dad's never had much use for him."

188

"Clancy's protective of Kyle. Kyle's protective of you," she said softly.

He nodded knowingly. "Anyway, Corey and I had a few words. Mostly over you, and we ironed out a few things. No major reconciliation mind you, but a start, which is more than we've ever made before."

"I'm glad," she said into the silence of his thoughts. It seemed a small thing, Corey's visit to Kyle, yet she marveled at the way it had touched T.K. Obviously, it was the timing that was so right.

"He leads me to believe you are his own personal missionary," T.K. said finally. "Why didn't you just tell me that, instead of all that nonsense about being just friends?"

Blushing, she murmured, "I don't know, T.K. It's hard for me to say the things that need to be said sometimes. I guess I was afraid you'd be scornful or something."

He studied her for a long time, his face thoughtful. "You make me ashamed," he said finally. "He's *my* brother and I guess I never really cared what became of his soul."

"There were other things you were trying to work through," she murmured. "Kyle told me about your mother." Feeling his shoulders stiffen, she added, "I wish you'd told me yourself."

"It's water under the bridge," he said and sounded as if he meant it. "About Corey, I told him he could have the museum."

"Your home?" Mandy's voice rose a little.

He nodded. "The roots of the place attract him. I guess it's kind of a line connecting him with Mother."

"T.K., that's really sweet of you," she said, trying not to think how similar the gesture was to his disastrous sharing of his inheritance. But his thoughts must have run in accord with hers, for he shook his head saying,

"No it wasn't. It wasn't even hard. The place

doesn't mean much to me. And anyway, it wasn't a gift. It was a businessmen's agreement. He's responsible for the upkeep, and he has to assure Mrs. Hart a home there for life. In return, I get complete ownership of the lodge property. I'm going to build a new house there, put in a pool and some fancy kennels right out the back door, if that's where Grand-dad wants them.

"Oh, and I get the girl." His arm hooked around her waist possessively.

"The girl?" She dared to smile with the questioning lift of a well-shaped eyebrow. "You drove a hard bargain."

He pulled her roughly onto his lap. "That isn't all. I told him we were going to change duties for a while. *He's* going on the road drumming up business and keeping in touch with the distributors while *I* sit in that plush office of his, pushing buttons and giving orders."

Intoxicated by the husky sound of his voice so near her ear, she said innocently, "That's funny. I never thought of you as the office type."

A grin of resignation slashed across his face. "What else is a fellow supposed to do when he's decided to settle down with the woman he loves? He can't go wandering around the country homesick all the time, can he?"

"You're acquiring a wife?"

The lamplight softened the gleam in his eyes. "That depends. Do you want to apply for the position?"

She melted into the warmth of his arms and gave her answer to his awaiting lips. "Yes."

ABOUT THE AUTHOR

SUSAN KIRBY is the 1984 winner of the Institute of American Writers' juvenile book award for her book, IKE & PORKER, published by Houghton Mifflin Co. She is the author of numerous romance novels, and her stories have appeared in magazines ranging from *Christian Life* to *Farm Wife News*. Aside from time spent writing romance novels, Susan is one of the organists for her church and enjoys reading, biking, swimming and gardening.

A Letter To Our Readers

Dear Reader:

In order that we might better contribute to your reading enjoyment, we would appreciate your taking a few minutes to respond to the following questions and return them to:

Editor, Serenade Books
The Zondervan Publishing House
1415 Lake Drive, S.E.
Grand Rapids, Michigan   49506

1. Did you enjoy reading HEART AFLAME?

   ☐ Very much. I would like to see more books by this author!
   ☐ Moderately
   ☐ I would have enjoyed it more if _____

2. Where did you purchase this book? _____

3. What influenced your decision to purchase this book?

   ☐ Cover   ☐ Back cover copy
   ☐ Title   ☐ Friends
   ☐ Publicity   ☐ Other _____

4. Would you be interested in reading other Serenade/Serenata or Serenade/Saga Books?

- [ ] Very interested
- [ ] Moderately interested
- [ ] Not interested

5. Please indicate your age range:

- [ ] Under 18
- [ ] 18–24
- [ ] 25–34
- [ ] 35–45
- [ ] 46–55
- [ ] Over 55

6. Would you be interested in a Serenade book club? If so, please give us your name and address:

Name _____

Occupation _____

Address _____

City _____ State _____ Zip _____

Serenade Saga books are inspirational romances in historical settings, designed to bring you a joyful, heart-lifting reading experience.

Serenade Saga books available in your local book store:

#1 SUMMER SNOW, Sandy Dengler
#2 CALL HER BLESSED, Jeanette Gilge
#3 INA, Karen Baker Kletzing
#4 JULIANA OF CLOVER HILL,
   Brenda Knight Graham
#5 SONG OF THE NEREIDS, Sandy Dengler
#6 ANNA'S ROCKING CHAIR,
   Elaine Watson
#7 IN LOVE'S OWN TIME,
   Susan C. Feldhake
#8 YANKEE BRIDE, Jane Peart
#9 LIGHT OF MY HEART, Kathleen Karr
#10 LOVE BEYOND SURRENDER,
   Susan C. Feldhake
#11 ALL THE DAYS AFTER SUNDAY,
   Jeanette Gilge
#12 WINTERSPRING, Sandy Dengler
#13 HAND ME DOWN THE DAWN,
   Mary Harwell Sayler
#14 REBEL BRIDE, Jane Peart
#15 SPEAK SOFTLY, LOVE, Kathleen Yapp
#16 FROM THIS DAY FORWARD, Kathleen Karr
#17 THE RIVER BETWEEN, Jacquelyn Cook
#18 VALIANT BRIDE, Jane Peart
#19 WAIT FOR THE SUN, Maryn Langer
#20 KINCAID OF CRIPPLE CREEK, Peggy Darty
#21 LOVE'S GENTLE JOURNEY, Kay Cornelius
#22 APPLEGATE LANDING, Jean Conrad

Serenade Serenata books are inspirational romances in contemporary settings, designed to bring you a joyful, heart-lifting reading experience.

Serenade Serenata books available in your local bookstore:

Watch for other books in both the *Serenade Saga* (historical) and *Serenade Serenata* (contemporary) series coming soon.